The *Ancient* Secrets of Life

Learn The Untold *Secrets* On How To Break The Strongholds of Your Past, Present, and Future.

Ruby Fleurcius

The *Ancient* Secrets of Life

Learn The Untold **Secrets** On How To Break The Strongholds
of Your Past, Present, and Future.

Spiritually Fit Publications
Ruby Fleurcius
581 N. Park Ave. Ste. #725
Apopka, FL 32704
321-312-0744

Published in the United States of America

ISBN: 978-0-9832075-5-9
$14.95

Table of Contents

DEDICATION

I dedicate this book to my Lord and Savior, who has so dearly blessed me beyond all measure. I thank Him for the information that He has poured into me so that I can bless you. It has taken a lot to get these **SECRETS** out of me, and I pray that it brings bountiful blessings in your life and the lives of the legacy that you will inspire. I would like to give a great big THANK YOU to everyone who contributed to or played their role in my life that led up to where I am today. I have received many apologies prior to the release of this book, and my forgiveness is extended in advance to those who were not able to ask for forgiveness. Every experience has provided a valuable lesson that I would not have received otherwise; therefore, I am grateful. I am so happy that I did not give up on me, even though the mockery was quite fierce; however, due to my heart, God's grace and mercy gave me a promise that "The last shall be first, and the first, shall be last." He also spoke into my heart that "My latter days would be greater than my former days, and it will come to pass." That was my promise, and that was the hope that rested in my heart with my unshakeable faith. Most people called me stubborn when I would not bow down to them. They also said that with enough pressure I would break; but, the one thing that they did not know is that I had a big SECRET! I had a PROMISE! I had a promise that was audibly spoken to me—so, no matter what obstacle life took me through, I held steadfast to that Audible Voice that had awakened me out of a dead sleep. I cannot say I never questioned life, because I did. However, I did not bow down to another God regardless of what people thought of me or called me. I take my spiritual relationship with God serious, and I can only give Him thanks for anointing me with a gift as such. Many are called, but few are chosen, is indeed a true statement; however, it is up to you to decide if you are going to choose to use your calling or allow your calling to choose to use you! May this book help you to take the setbacks in your life and make something beautiful. Holy Spirit speak to those who have an open ear to hear. In the Mighty Name of Jesus. Amen.

INTRODUCTION

The Ancient Secrets of Life is a Spiritual Navigational tool used to build individuals mentally, physically, mentally, emotionally, and spiritually to propel them into their destiny. In all that we do, say, and become, we all need some form of guidance; and, that's where **The Ancient Secrets of Life** comes in to help one to expand his or her territory. There are many lessons that we must learn, and there are many lessons that we overlook, which I consider a Blessing. Make no mistake about it, life is also a journey that we will all take, and there is no avoiding it—it's just a matter of getting through it; whether we fight our way through or pray our way through is totally up to each individual. Most often, we look down on prayer, push it to the side, or avoid it all together; but, if one would find the time to collect their small prayers daily—we would be amazed at the number of small miracles or blessings we throw away that could help us through life or help someone in need. Better yet, is it not the prayers of a righteous man that availeth much? (James 5:16). Does prayer not give us the ability to walk by faith and not by sight? (2 Corinthians 5:7). Does the Bible not tell us to devote ourselves to prayer, being watchful and thankful? (Colossians 4:2). It is hard to see the value of one prayer until it's collected in an abundant amount—1 prayer has little value; 10 prayers have more value than 1; 100 prayers have more value than 10, etc. Regardless of how we look at a prayer, they do add up, and they work! That is really something to think about, right? As we get down to the nitty-gritty, how many small blessings does life leave behind for us, and we push them to the side, or walk right over them? How many Breadcrumbs fall from our Master's table, but we are too good to pick them up? These are the same questions that we will be revisiting to bring life to our present day situations, circumstances, and events that are depleting our Powerhouse. We will all have our time of enslavement where something or someone binds us; and for this reason, **The Ancient Secrets of Life** shares biblical secrets that have gone unnoticed until now.

In life, we deal with success and failure, but in between the two, there are hidden blessings that often go overlooked. It is the small blessings that make this Book a prerequisite to attaining true success. **The Ancient Secrets of Life** believes that genuine success is doing what we have been destined to do with the ultimate freedom and prosperity from within. Living a life out of purpose or in bondage creates a life that's full of limitations and excuses that hinder our ability to embrace our purpose or passion. We have been conditioned to think that success is hard to achieve or difficult to come by, when it is not hard or difficult at all. In fact, all that is needed is a true understanding of how to make our **Prayers** useful to empower or fuel our belief system. And, this is where **The Ancient Secrets of Life** comes in to take you on a journey out of your Egypt, through the wilderness, and into your Promise Land by sharing principles, insights, ideas, and concepts that will keep success chasing after you. Once this process is mastered, winning becomes second nature, or better yet, instinctual when we focus on doing the right thing, with the right people, at the right time. It is said that timing is everything, and now is the time for you to indulge in "The Ancient Secrets of Life."

CHAPTER 1

The Secrets of "Our Truth"

As we are surrounded by the fame and fortune of the rich and famous or the well to do, and we paint a glorious picture of going to school to become educated; we do not often hear about the low down dirty struggles of what it has cost us to become who we are today. Most of us are too ashamed to tell anyone about what it has taken us to get what we have, what we had to go through to get what we have, what we had to sacrifice to get what we have, or what we have to continue to do to keep what we have. We would dare not tell anyone that we got through on a wing and a prayer! We dare not tell anyone that we are still living on a wing and a prayer. We dare not tell "OUR TRUTH!"

The cost of what we have today has cost us more than we could ever tell anyone, and sometimes we may have to go to our grave holding that secret in our heart.....those are some of the costs that we may or may not ever tell. It is that edge of destruction that pushed us out of our comfort zone to do something that we've never done before, that edge that caused us to say something that we've never said before or that edge that caused us to become someone that we've never imagined becoming to bring forth that Greatness. It is the COST of the struggle that really creates its value, and the struggles of life will never get its grafted power if it's not accounted for, or if it does not cost us anything. Invaluable blessings cannot be left around town unaccounted for, or they will lose their power because it will not receive the respect that it rightly deserves! This is exactly why we have those who are hungry for success, jumping from one thing to the next without any real achievement, or those who are willing to do anything to paint a superficial picture of real achievement, with nothing to show for it. For example, if they died tomorrow, they would not have a legacy to leave behind; and after the money is spent, they would be easily forgotten about—there is no form of impact what-so-ever, they are just existing! Those are the ones who have a tendency to half-do projects, never completing anything, including jobs, relationships, tasks; those are usually the ones that will sell-out at the drop of a dime; and those are also the ones that are always late, lazy, irresponsible, blame others, prayerless, co-dependent and the list goes on. What we will find is that those are usually the strongholds that drain our power, which are the key contributors to blocked prayers, blocked blessings, and a blocked life.

Now, my question is, "Are you willing to pay the cost to become a successful, fervent prayer? Are you willing to do what most people are not willing to do? Are you willing to gather up your losses, and come clean with your atrocities?

And, are you willing to pray your way TO IT, pray your way THROUGH IT, or pray your way OUT OF IT?"

We have been conditioned to think that praying is difficult, when it is not hard or difficult at all. In fact, all that is needed is a true understanding of what prayer is and why we need to pray. For the most part, everyone has a desire for something—for some, it's success, good health, peace, happiness, and for others it's a good husband, wife, or children. We have some who pimp God to become famous, rich, or to live a life of luxury, etc. This perception of blessings is an illusion, giving us false hope, and an inaccurate view to those who are not as fortunate. To a great degree, we are striving for something we truly do not understand; however, due to our lack of understanding, self-deception plays a vital role in our feelings of failure or unworthiness when material gain is not attained. Therefore, let's get a good understanding of true success in the areas that we are gifted before we move on.

True success is "Our Truth." It is doing what we have been destined to do with the ultimate freedom desired. True success is FREEDOM, not money. No, I am not opposed to money, but if our desire for success in a particular area of our lives is driven by money or to get rich quick, then we will miss the entire point of overcoming a STRONGHOLD. As a part of **The Ancient Secrets of Life**, your focus will not be to pray for wealth, fame, or fortune; it will be to bring forth your talents, gifts, and abilities from within. Your talents, gifts, and abilities are a part of you—they are your birthright. Therefore, you cannot pursue something that is already there; but you must protect that which is already. The only way to safeguard them is to become prayerful and learn the ancient secrets of the past, present, and future to ensure that you do not take your giftings or blessings for granted.

Remember Esau, who sold his birthright for a bowl of lentil stew? Just in case you don't know the story, "*Now Jacob cooked a stew; and Esau came in from the field, and he was weary. And Esau said to Jacob, "Please feed me with that same red stew, for I am weary." Therefore, his name was called Edom. But Jacob said, "Sell me your birthright as of this day." And Esau said, "Look, I am about to die; so what is this birthright to me?" Then Jacob said, "Swear to me as of this day." So he swore to him, and sold his birthright to Jacob. And Jacob gave Esau bread and stew of lentils; then he ate and drank, arose, and went his way. Thus, Esau despised his birthright."* Genesis 25:29-34

Esau, the son of Isaac, had no value in his birthright (promises from God for the future); as a result, he forfeited his inheritance to his younger brother Jacob—selling himself short in the end for instant gratification. Hebrews 12:16 advises us, "Not to be godless like Esau, who for a single meal sold his inheritance rights as the oldest son." For that reason, when securing a relationship with our Spiritual Self, we may not be able to conceive the value of our blessings today, but there will be value tomorrow as well! Most often we would look down on a small blessing or gifting because it may not appear as if it would be much right now; however, we should not cheat ourselves, just acknowledge it, pray about it, and accept our birthright through faith.

Now, my question is, "What has been holding you back from being successful in the areas that you so desire?" Or, "What are the excuses you have been using to justify not doing what you need to do?" I am presenting these questions to get you to think about some of the obstacles preventing you from protecting what you have inside of you. There are two ways to break the STRONGHOLD that's within you:

1. Sell your soul through pride, envy, arrogance, jealousy, or betrayal.
2. Pray as you discover and use the untapped potential that's inside of you.

According to **The Ancient Secrets of Life**, discovering, and using the untapped potential inside of you will be the way to break any form of STRONGHOLD, secure your success, and open the door to spiritual empowerment. This type of information will not be what you are accustomed to; however, I am opening up to the World to share **The Ancient Secrets of Life** on a personal level! I think on a different level for a reason, I speak on a different level for a reason, and I write differently for a reason; therefore, if you allow me to activate the Law of Reciprocity in this area—I promise that I will take you to a level of Greatness that will bless you for generations to come. The Wisdom that I have received from God states, "Mind Power + Will (soul) power + Emotional power + Spiritual power = Success and Wholeness." Remember, this is already within you; I am just going to share with you how to use it or how to maximize it to your benefit through the Power of Prayer.

According to 1 Corinthians 7:7, God has given everyone their own abilities, talents, or gifts; and, since we have different gifts according to the grace given to us, we are supposed to exercise them accordingly. In so many words, you are a true success story. In order to bring it into reality, you must be able to use the gifts that God has given you to bless and help others with a sense of purpose, direction, and total commitment. This is where I come in to provide the **Hidden Secrets** as well as the incentive to get you up and moving toward your destiny. In order to do this, I am going to take you back to the Bible to take a journey through Egypt to give you a bird's-eye view of The Children of Israel's journey in 3 phases:

SECRET PHASE 1:
We will take a journey through Egypt, dealing thoroughly with the Slavery and Bondage Experience; which will be considered the Preparation Phase of Life.

SECRET PHASE 2:
We will take a journey through the Desert with the Children of Israel to Experience what they were dealing with during their Trials, Training, and Testing Phase of Life.

SECRET PHASE 3:
We will experience a taste of what it feels like to be in the Perfecting, Polishing, and Perseverance Phase of Life that leads us to our Ultimate Destiny.

If your dream, vision, or whatever you are praying for is worth the journey, please keep in mind that material gain can be taken at a moment's notice. However, the information, knowledge, or wisdom that you obtain at this point is irrevocable, unless you choose NOT to receive it. Better yet, the same applies to your success in whatever area you so desire; if you recall, "YOUR TRUTH" comes from within. I am challenging you to believe in the gift or talent that is inside of you without any limitations. Listen to me, in order to cultivate your true **POWER**, don't worry about whether other people believe in you, whether it is right or wrong, whether you deserve it or not, or whether you have a gift or talent. If you are reading this book right now, "Just know that it is there." Here are some "DO NOTs" to remember about **The Ancient Secrets of Life**:

- You do not have to overwork yourself to become successful in your prayers—your gift will make room for you and will set you before men in high places, Proverbs 18:16.
- You do not need a man or woman to support you when you pray. No good thing does He withhold from those who walk uprightly, Proverbs 84:11.
- You do not have to be creative to pray effectively.
- You do not have to be born rich to reap the fruits of your prayers.
- You do not have to be lucky to become blessed or have the favor of God hovering over your life.
- You do not have to have a degree to have a fervent prayer.
- You do not have to be smart to understand what moves God to bring wisdom your way.

- You do not have to be worldly to be able to get what you want with the Power of Prayer.
- You do not have to be deceptive to make your prayers effective.
- You do not have to feel limited when you seek God's face and not His hand.
- You do not have to sacrifice your soul to become blessed.

CHAPTER 2

The Secrets of Praying

Finding loopholes in life is a common point of misdirection when it comes down to mastering a strategy on how to succeed at what we are good at. In order to stay on track, it is imperative that we do a follow-up on ourselves, believe in ourselves, and pray. If we do not make it our business to do any of these things, they will soon elude us until the next week, the next month, and then the next year. The cycle will repeat itself if we do not make a conscious effort to change how we look at or deal with the way in which we use our prayers and how we apply our faith. Furthermore, when we try to find a loophole or the easy way out, we often fail at our efforts because we are designed to strategize, pray, and believe. Most often, these are overlooked traits that help us fine-tune our goals or desires, instead of having our goals or desires fine-tune us. As a matter of fact, the first step to mastering a strategy is to simply read our goals daily, evaluate them weekly, and pray for Divine Guidance as we focus on the objective and not the obstacle. If you are falling short in this area, don't worry—in the next chapter, we are going to heal those afflictions and put a little pep in your step to ensure that you are able to stick to your strategies, pray, and believe in yourself a little more.

Most often, we fall short because we stop believing in ourselves. Of course, we would never tell anyone this; but deep within—in some way, we have lost hope. When you feel as if all hope is gone, just remember that your hope is still there as long as you don't let go of it. As a matter of fact, making the extra effort to hold on to your hope will supernaturally spark a greater hope that can only come from within you. How do you embrace the greater hope? That's a great question. The answer is, "Love the skin that you are in." Love everything about you, the good and the not so good, the positive and the not so positive, the pretty and the not so pretty things about you and the things in your life. In so many words, you have to appreciate who you are and where you are, in order to embrace the greatness that's longing to come out of you. Start loving the life you live, and live the life you love; this will ensure that you do not provide a breeding ground for anything superficial.

Superficial achievement is recognized by the constant excuse of not having enough time or the lack of commitment. This type of individual will always talk about what they are going to do, but never do it. Frankly, waiting, wishing, and hoping for great things, most often will not do us a bit of good if we constantly waste or mismanage our time. However, a real achievement comes when we become committed and prayerful about what we are doing; and prioritizing our time while including a little prayer will increase our productivity and consistency. Take a moment to calculate the time you spend doing things that keep you busy wasting time. How much time do you spend watching TV, on the phone, or doing things that are not productive or fruitful? Yes, that is something to think about, huh! More importantly, take some time out to seize the small opportunities that happen on a daily basis that will surely add up over a period of time. Trust me, time is on your side, and it will work for you if you pray about it and work it! Now, let me show you how to do just that....

Why Pray?

It is one thing to just pray, but it is another thing to know why we are praying, what we are praying for, where we are going to pray, how we are going to pray, and when we are going to pray.

Prayer is our intimate conversation with God about any and everything. We often use prayer to confess our sins, to ask for forgiveness, to ask for help with a weakness, to fight temptation, to pray for the sick, to pray for our enemies, to pray for guidance, to make requests to fill a need, want, or desire, and it is used in spiritual warfare. It is fair to say that we do have different levels of prayer such as the smaller level, medium level, high level, and deep level of prayer—they are all governed based on our level of need. If one is battling with a Demon, a small prayer is not going to work—that is going to take deep prayer, and one does not need a deep prayer if they need help looking for a lost item.

There are a few components of prayer that we should take into consideration, but it's not set in stone....our prayer is a personal conversation between our Heavenly Father and us; and if we desire to worship Him during our prayer time, do it. It really depends on our personality, but the leading of the Spirit will nudge us when worship is a must. However, it's to our benefit to give praise, thanks, and repent daily; we need it! If there is a need to intercede on behalf of someone, do it! If there is a need for guidance, ask for it! If there is a personal request, make it!

Prayer is our time to commune or have a conversation with our Creator to ensure that His creation is okay. Besides, if He created us, He knows our needs, wants, and desires; however, He has given us a free will to make choices. He did not create robots; therefore, we must acknowledge our own needs, wants, and desires, while making our request known to Him, so that He can intercede on our behalf. It seems simple.....so, why is life so complicated? If we had a perfect life, if we did not have a need, if we did not experience any form of hurt, if we had our way with everything, then we would have no need for Him. We lost that perfect life in the Garden of Eden—the trust is out the window on that one! The Power of Temptation is flowing through our veins, even if we do not like to admit it. Now, we must trust ourselves enough to seek His face and not His hand, especially when it comes down to praying our way through life. Matthew 7-8 tells us: "Ask, and it shall be given you; seek, and ye shall find; knock, and it shall be opened unto you: For every one that asketh receiveth; and he that seeketh findeth; and to him that knocketh it shall be opened." Therefore, if we think for a minute that prayer does not work, we must think again!

We must keep ourselves and our family prayed up, because it only takes a second to ruin a good thing, and it takes less than that to lose control of ourselves; therefore, we must be able to think on our feet without allowing our emotions to rule and reign. When we are true to ourselves, it opens the door to become real about who we are with limits and boundaries, and not a person that cannot rule over his or her own soul.

What does God expect from us? I will gladly answer that question: the expectation that God has for us, is a continued praise and thank you. It does not require much—a brief moment in the day really adds up. If we take a few minutes of prayer in the morning, afternoon, and evening, I promise that it will take less time than a conversation with our BFF, our favorite TV show, checking our emails, etc. All I am saying is that we should not forget the One who gives us the strength to do what we do without giving it a second thought!

CHAPTER 3

The Secrets of Belief

Faith is powerful, and it works! There is nothing magical about the power of faith; it is your attitude of belief that generates the power, skill, and energy needed to produce results. When you believe you can do it, the "HOW TO" develops. On the other hand, when you lack faith in yourself and your abilities, limits are placed on God automatically; and, the one thing that He will not do is override your will! God will meet you at the level of your expectation; furthermore, looking at something from a distance does not provide you with the intricate details of being up close and personal. In order to accurately assess anything in life, you need to know the details. Making decisions without having the facts presented to you will eventually cause you to make a few major mistakes in your life. Yes, you can learn from your mistakes, but some mistakes can be avoided. It is good to ask questions, and it's okay to know the details when it comes down to you and your well-being; because most bad decisions are derived out of impatience, the lack of information, or the lack of prayer. Just take a little more time to get the facts. As a rule of thumb, approach every situation and circumstance with the promises of God, release the power of faith from within you, and be patient while standing firm, and sooner or later everything will fall into place according to the will of God.

The primary culprit of missed opportunities is living in a fantasy world, expecting everything to be totally perfect in an imperfect world. Fantasies are not a bad thing! Fantasies can be considered a lot of things; however, fantasies are not a goal, passion, or purpose. It is an ILLUSION of perfection that is used to nourish the people, places, and things that are hoped for. However, an unrestrained fantasy does not have enough power to change your life, nor does it have enough power to provide a disciplined lifestyle. It only has enough power to fill a psychological need temporarily to keep your hope alive or create a web of deception. Yes, there is a positive and a negative side; however, for the sake of this book, we are going to focus on the positive. Just remember, fantasies are designed to give you hope and not an easy way out of working for what you want. If you want to make your goal, passion, or purpose a reality—simply make a difference with imperfect opportunities that will make a positive impact on the lives of others.

Living a life full of regret is not an easy task. It takes work to truly value yourself and when you do, it will draw success out of you. You may not have a lot of money, but if you take the extra time to appreciate the great person that you are, there is no limit to what you can achieve. More often than not, distractions will come, but they will soon fade away if you stir your own passion instead of the passion that someone else thinks you should have. Start analyzing your life and evaluate whether your life is living up to your standards or whether you are just settling for less. You know the desires of your heart; besides, your instincts will guide you to what's right for you anyway. That's why it is very important to follow your instincts as you take your innermost desires and strive to make them a reality. Remember, no one or nothing owes you anything; but you owe it to the world to be the best at whatever you do, say, and become—doing everything in the Spirit of Excellence. Just remember that you are your legacy, simply write the vision, pray over it, and make it count for something.

Believe it or not, every blessing count—it is up to you to create a win-win situation out of it. At the beginning of my journey, I was judged by my small blessings, I was rejected because of my small blessings, I was overlooked because my small blessings were not good enough, I was mistreated because of my small blessings, and I was abused because of my small blessings; nevertheless, I found my true POWER in the small blessings because I prayed, exercised my faith, and never stopped giving love, hope, and peace to those around me. And, now that the tables have turned, as they always do—it is those same people that judged, rejected, overlooked, mistreated, and abused what I had to offer, that are now **GLEANING** from those same small blessings. For that reason, we should never underestimate the Power that is hidden in the small blessings that do not appear as much, because most often that is indeed our blessing in disguise.

This brings me back to a pivotal moment that I will never forget as long as I live: After recovering from a minor stroke,

I had a few setbacks health-wise; however; I was invited to an event, and upon leaving I decided to take a plate to go. This particular individual intentionally tried to serve me literally the left-over burned crumbs of macaroni & cheese from the bottom of a pan that she had taken from underneath the table that roaches came out of. She did not know that I saw that; but, I politely refused it! It was a big to-do because I would not take it; she felt as if I was too good. I felt under no circumstances should she serve me that. Here we are with two different mindsets. **Her mindset:** She thinks that I am too good to eat the scraps from the bottom of the pan. She thinks that I am better than everybody. **My mindset:** I have always given you the best. I have always treated you like a Queen. I have given your child anything that she has ever requested from me since the day that she was born. I have trained and mentored your child with the secrets of my wisdom that she will carry on for the rest of her life. I have given you fish to eat. I have taught you how to fish. The meal that you are feeding me the crumbs from, is it not I, that taught you how to get it? Is it not from my wisdom that you glean, is it not from my ideas that you have used to purchase what you have fed everyone else, but the one person that would give you the shirt off their back? Is it not because of me that you now provide for your household, and I ask for nothing in return but for you to succeed in life? Have I not been your shoulder to cry on? Have I ever mistreated you one day in your entire life? Have I ever said one discouraging word to you? Have I ever given you any reason to make you feel that I would not be there for you? Have I not shown you unconditional love? Would I not go hungry so you could eat? Is it not I that you should have fed first, is it not I that you

Chapter 3 | Ruby Fleurcius

should have blessed your seed with? Is it not I that you should have blessed your future with? Is it not I that you should have shown compassion to due to my frail condition? The only reason that you have found to feed me the contaminated crumbs from the bottom of a pan is that you are not happy with the fact that I have been marked for greatness; and I hold myself to a higher standard mentally, physically, emotionally, and spiritually. I know you secretly desire to be where I am, and you don't understand why God has chosen me among all the women in the world for this task, and you are doing this to show me how it feels to be considered less than. Well, it is not my fault if you chose not to succeed in the area that you are gifted in, because I have given you every opportunity to succeed in life. You are sitting under great wisdom, but you refused it. The ones that I gave less wisdom, less mentoring, and less everything, did more with what I gave them; and, every single one of them are professionals in their field; and they are absolutely grateful. You have instant access to a fountain to build any dream that you could ever dream, but you refused it—your pride will not allow you to embrace it. People would give anything to be where you are, but there is no value—you have the nerve to humiliate me in my weakest moment. I tell you, when I am weak, then I am strong, only envy could cause a person to treat someone as such. I forgive you, not just for your sake, but for mine as well; and, this is the very reason why God has chosen me for this mission—I am quick to forgive. What everyone considered as the greatest weakness, God considered the greatest strength; therefore, granting me an anointing of Supernatural Wisdom that penetrates the heart of those who dare to believe.

I had never been so insulted in my entire life regarding a situation as such. Although I am very picky about my food; however, in my opinion, regarding food, that was the lowest. At first, I could not get that situation out of my head; because through her eyes, she saw nothing wrong. She saw that I was the problem. I accepted total responsibility for my role in the situation; however, I just choose not to eat that way, and I choose not to live like that. To each his own, but that is just a choice for me, and I am entitled to that. I prayed asking God how I could create a win-win situation out of something like that. He kept saying that I had it. I was confused a little, but when I took my emotions out of that situation, then I was able to see clearly. God was telling me that I had to gather the Nuggets of Wisdom that were being left behind as a lesson or a tool, discard the emotions that I did not need, and move on to regain my POWER. For me, I firmly believe in creating a win-win situation out of everything; and, it is that situation that gave birth to the invaluable information that you are reading right now.

It took someone that I love dearly, to try to serve me the crumbs of Roach Infested Macaroni & Cheese, in a time of my life when I was not feeling at my best, to draw the Power of Belief out of me. This is indeed a Win-Win situation that will save and inspire the lives of millions to the end of time. It cannot get any better than that! Now, that's an affliction to laugh about; what was once my favorite dish, can no longer touch my lips—that's how easily we can become scarred for life.

The scars of life, we can't get away from them, and no one is immune—if we live long enough, it will come knocking on our door. Hopefully, we will have a band-aid;

but if not, what do we do? The scars of our afflictions can have enough power to make us cry and wallow in self-pity; however, it has the same amount of power to give us something to smile about. If we can learn how to embrace the true greatness that we possess from within, we can turn that scar around and create a win-win situation! The key to our scars will be how we view them—we can see it as an obstacle or an opportunity; nevertheless, it will be ultimately our choice whether or not we give our POWER away or believe that our POWER will sustain us.

If our goal is to experience the ultimate bliss of freedom, we must find a way to stop groaning, whining, and complaining. We must start looking at life as a training process; every life lesson that we are served may not be a good one, it may not be up to our standards, and it may not be to our liking—the key is, what are we going to do with it? What are we learning from it? Who are we helping? What are the benefits? I am not saying that we will not shed a few tears over that badly served lesson, but I am saying, "Wipe those tears away, brush the dust off, pray about it, learn from the experience, and follow the path of wisdom toward greatness." **Word of Caution**: Make sure you are not intentionally sowing bad seeds of havoc. Or, trying to repay a badly sown seed back with havoc. The Law of Karma is in full effect for our seeds or deeds, in and out of season; therefore, it is always best to keep our hands blessed at all times.

Are the little blessings not as important as the big ones? Little blessings and big blessings carry the same amount of weight when it comes down to the acknowledgment of what it is. There are times when we totally forget about the little blessings that take place on a daily basis—not realizing that the little blessings prepare the way for the big ones. Most often, we miss out on our blessings because we don't expect them. The key word here is expectation. Trust me; expectancy has enough power to create a day of total bliss or put a damper on the brightest man's day. Regardless of how big or small, our blessing is—if it is not recognized, it will have no apparent value. As a matter of fact, we are just as responsible for receiving our blessing as we are for **not** getting one; therefore, it is imperative that we become open and ready to giving as well as receiving.

CHAPTER 4

The Secrets Behind Religiosity

Religion has been around since the beginning of time—it is indeed as ancient as it could possibly get. But, for some odd reason, some of us fail to understand the word Religion outside of the Church. Therefore, it is my reasonable service to give one a better understanding of it, to ensure that the secret doors of our prayers will effectively open for us.

First and foremost, Religion is derived from the word Religio; which means relating back to, our roots, what binds us, what ties us down, or what keeps us obligated; therefore, anything that we relate back to codependently can become our religion, positively or negatively. Can religion really help us? The answer is "Yes." If that is what we are looking for. Religion is designed to control, manipulate, and place us in a box to judge the outsiders who are not a part of the acultic segregated belief system. In my opinion, religion causes us to point fingers, without us realizing that there are three fingers pointing back at us; therefore, we must always look from within ourselves asking the question, "Is it me, O'Lord?"

This ensures that we are able to show Universal Love to all mankind, regardless of creed or deed!

Throughout my journey in life, the key to living a fulfilled life is to develop a relationship with your Heavenly Father, first; then a relationship with self, and then on to building a relationship with others. If we get this out of order, chaos will soon follow in religion, in a relationship, or in life, period; and we will go back to where we started, looking for another form of Religion to fill that void from within. Trust me, there is a certain order in the Universe—for example, in the morning, we will never see the sunset before the sunrise, we will never see the sun rise from the west or the sun set in the east—the day that we see that happening, we have a serious problem. Relationships bring people together, whereas Religion divides us, causing us to look down on people, places, and things opposed to building them up. According to Proverbs 6:12-14, it says *"A worthless person, a wicked man, Is the one who walks with a false mouth, Who winks with his eyes, who signals with his feet, Who points with his fingers; Who with perversity in his heart devises evil continually, Who spreads strife."*

Religion creates biased favoritism that divides us, opposed to bringing us together as one big family. And, that is why we must develop a RELATIONSHIP with our Heavenly Father and not come to Him with protocol, procedures, or routines—He wants our heart, He wants us to relate to Him, and He wants our spirit to connect with His Holy Spirit. When Religion is presented in our lives, it is designed to train us in some way, because we will always appear right in our own eyes based on our belief system. However, if we look at the situation from a different perspective, it is a possibility that we would be able to see something a little different. That is why it takes something as small as a thorn in our flesh to draw "IT" out, due to the fact that we will miss the point if there is no pain attached to it. In so many words, Religion is designed to betray us, to enable us to learn the value of having a personal relationship with our Heavenly Father.

As a Nugget of Wisdom, the big things are always evident; however, the simple little things get overlooked by the arrogant, who do not pay attention! Keep in mind that when we are scarred or afflicted, it's a testimony in the making—just ask Joseph. In the Old Testament, Joseph was the 11th of the twelve sons of Jacob, the grandson of Isaac, and the great-grandson of Abraham. He was the 1st born of his mother, Rachel. He was obviously the most favored child, and Jacob, his father, did not make it a secret. He gave Joseph a coat of many colors, to reveal that he was very special. Was he wrong? In my opinion, Jacob's approach to favoritism of one child over another, making favoritism blatantly obvious among his sons is definitely wrong. Does God favor one person over another? The answer is "Yes." Is He wrong? The answer is no. Why do I say Jacob's wrong, and I am saying God is not. The answer is that God provides everyone an opportunity for an equal amount of favor.

God has set in motion certain Laws that will reign on the just and the unjust alike that will sway favor in our direction, if we learn the secrets of how favoritism works. Seed, time, and harvest happen to be one of them. God is not partial, He loves us all regardless of who gave birth to us, and He stands for righteousness regardless of who we are or what we have. He loves us if we are rich or poor, successful or unsuccessful, smart or not smart, healthy or sick, talented or untalented, However, that is not what Jacob was sowing among his sons—according to scripture, he never once made a coat of any sort for any of his other sons. What a father does for one child, he must be willing to do for them all. The key word here is WILLING, and that was not the case. He was sowing discord in his own house.

He did not let go of that spirit of favoritism that divided him from his brother Esau, his mother Rebekah, and his father, Isaac. Although he did deal with the trickster mentality; but, he allowed his emotions to cloud his sense of good judgment. Anyway, before I move on, let me drop a few nuggets on this Trickster Mentality. I am going to make it quick because this story is about Joseph and not Jacob. However, Jacob picked up this trickster mentality from his mother, he tricked his brother twice out of his blessing, and he deceived his own father; who knows how long Jacob had been tricking people. I would say that he was a smooth operator to trick his own father, a blind man. In my opinion, that's a good trickster, I would say—blind or not, a mother or father, knows the voice, feel, sound, and everything about their child; and, if there was some residing doubt—there was a reason why his father, a Man of God would second-guess himself. That would only mean that Jacob was just that GOOD! God had to put a stop to Jacob's waywardness by allowing him to meet his match in Genesis 29:13, where his uncle Laban tricks him with something he really wanted with all his heart, and that was Rachel. What did he get as his treat? Leah! He labored 7 years thinking that he was getting Rachel as his wife, and got Leah—he could not give her back because he had already slept with her. What a way to get a baby, right? It happens all too often? Our Seeds of Deceit

Chapter 4 | Ruby Fleurcius

are all over the place left and right! How is it that we think that we would somehow profit from it? Women are intentionally getting pregnant trying to trap men. Men are intentionally getting women pregnant trying to trap them. Women get pregnant from one man to ensnare a different man—these are the deceitful seeds that are sown day in and day out. It's amazing how we get innocent children involved in a web of deception, and they have to pay the price of their parent's debaucheries.

Jacob was no longer the deceiver; he was now being deceived, and he did not like it not one bit. In this particular situation, in Genesis 29:20-23, he had to slave another 7 years for Rachel, and she was still barren; therefore, he had children with a woman that he did not want, a woman that he did not love, a woman that he semi-despised for tricking him, and a woman that he could not see that God was truly blessing. In my opinion, she was more blessed than all of his wives, even if she was not the favorite one. God was showing Leah favor for a reason—it was not her fault that she got caught up in their trickery and debauchery, but Jacob could not see beyond what he wanted! He could not fully despise her because she was the mother of his children; and, he was indeed guilty of the same trickery as well; therefore, God rewarded her with 6 children, and she gave birth to Judah, the lineage of Jesus. (Matthew 1:2-3).

Now, getting back to Joseph, his other sons did not feel the sting of the rejection until Joseph came along. And, Jacob intentionally wanted to make Joseph feel as if he was better than his other sons. Jacob spoiled Joseph, putting him up on a pedestal, educating him very well, while his brothers tended the flocks, how insulting! In my opinion, that would put a bad taste in any child's mouth. Then this little spoiled brat is a little tattletale, snitching on everyone. Can you imagine having a little child get you, a grown man, in trouble?

Now they were able to really feel the neglect that their mother felt, and his brothers only reacted according to how their father made their mother feel; all the years that he placed Joseph's mother over theirs. That coat of many colors was their breaking point for the many facades of favoritism that was taking place in the family—Jacob was allowing his house to become divided once again because he could not keep his favoritism of his children in check. Every time his brothers looked at that coat, it made them angry as their hatred brewed according to Genesis 37:4. Then, Joseph has the nerves, to start bragging about it in Genesis 37:5. To know that you are the favorite child is one thing, to brag about being the favorite child is another, and to treat your children differently based on their status of favoritism creates a whole new ball game. In my opinion, Jacob did not care if they became angry, because he contributed to the dilemma, instead of learning from the situation that took place between him and his brother—he pretended as if it did not happen. And, he allowed the cycle to continue.

As the favoritism, jealousy, instigating, and sibling rivalry spiraled out of control, the ultimate plan was to kill Joseph. Can you imagine how parents contribute to sisters and brothers wanting to kill each other over one parent loving one child more than the other? Can you imagine being scarred for life, because your mother or father did not love you like they love your brother or sister? Can you imagine longing to measure up to someone that you know that would outshine you in the heart of your mother or father? That's what favoritism does to a child who has to compete for the love of a mother or father, who will never love them enough to compare with a child who holds their heart. They were willing to do anything to make the pain go away, and if that meant getting rid of Joseph—that's what they had to do; but, that was not in God's plan. However, as an alternative, Joseph was sold to slave traders for ½ of a pound of silver. They went back to their father with that trickster mentality, along with the coat of many colors saying that he was attacked and killed on the road by a wild animal. Is that not Déjà vu? Why am I talking about favoritism so much? Favoritism, favoritism, favoritism, we cannot get away from it!

Joseph was taken to Egypt by the slave traders where he was sold to Potiphar as a field slave. Favoritism, again! As time passed, he became a slave in charge of Potiphar's house, a prisoner, overseer of the prison, and then 2nd in charge of all of Egypt. Favoritism, again! As you may have read a number of times, by Joseph becoming 2nd in charge of all of Egypt, he was able to save his father and his entire family from a famine that swept the land. Favoritism, again! This is a perfect example of how our afflictions have a greater purpose, and why we should never underestimate the Power of Our Prayers; therefore, we must become grateful in all things because we never know when things may change.

Unfortunately, there was another test, the Children of Israel went from a time of plentiful blessings with Joseph to experiencing great hardship after he died. It is amazing how

God preserved them, grew them into a great nation, and then afflicted them to test their faith while enhancing their growth.

As time went on, they began to cry out to God, but their crying out became a groan out of misery causing them to become angry, resentful, frustrated, insecure, and unhappy. They did have a promise from God, but they were not equipped or properly trained to possess the promise. In so many words, they were not ready! There are times when we think that we are ready for something, but we are not; especially when the value hasn't been established yet. God firmly believes in training, molding, and testing. He will not allow us to possess the promise to fail at it miserably.

Real Reason

I have introduced favoritism to you early on in this book for a reason. Okay, I admit this story is not just about Joseph, and it's not just about a story out of the Bible—this is about the reality of what's really taking place right now in our homes, on the job, and with our friends. Favoritism is everywhere. Favoritism affected God's chosen people and it still an epidemic for us now. I am not talking about the favoritism of God; I am talking about the favoritism that's going on behind closed doors. We have lost control of our homes because our children have learned how to play one parent against the other to get what they want, parents are manipulating children to become little spies and bullies, hurting others just to get rewarded with favor. Where is the love? Somehow we have confused the word love with favor. On the job, we get in good with our supervisors to receive favor—forget about integrity, as our title says favorite employee, anything goes. Don't say the magic words: Free FOOD! Food and Favor, I guess I would say food equals favor, right? The best way to get a smile is through food? Is that the cliché? And, please do not have a party without food, or it would be the worst party ever, right? Is that why it's better to have party favors? There are a lot of things that take place on the job to promote favoritism—each situation is unique, just know that they do take place; it's a matter of choice for all involved.

When we appear as if we have money, we receive instant favoritism; but, if we look like we don't have money, we get overlooked. When we live in a huge house, everyone wants to come by and visit; but if we live in a shack, would we not be worthy of that same visit? No favoritism there....not good enough. If we drive a fancy car, we get a stare; but, if we drive a little hooptie, we are good for the favorite laugh of the day. Who has the favorite house, car, outfit, etc.; that's our society today. Favoritism is everywhere. We have lost our sense of being. Society is dictating. Friends are dictating. Social Pressure is everywhere, where is your voice? Where is the Voice of God, can you even hear Him speak? Can you? Is your favor broken? Can you find the Trail of Secrets? I am dropping them all over the place, are you picking them up? Hold on; let me drop the real one.

Favoritism has broken us because we have gotten it confused and misdirected. The Favoritism from God is the real intent of the word, but we have channeled the energy in the wrong direction. The energy should be channeled from God, ourselves, and then outwardly through the Power of Prayer. However, we have misdirected it by short-circuiting favor by channeling it to ourselves first, and then outwardly. When our favor is short-circuited, it is short-lived, period. That is WRONG! In my opinion, that is so, so, OUT OF ORDER! That is why we have fights, confusion, chaos, anger, etc. in our homes, on the job, and even in the church, over what? Favoritism status! It is misdirected energy.

The Favoritism of God cannot compare to any other favoritism on the face of this earth. When we receive favoritism that's not Divinely ordained, it comes with conditions, and when the conditions are not met, the favor is removed; therefore, resulting in a few short-circuits causing great disappointment, hurt, and shame. That is how we lose our POWER and our EFFECTIVENESS. Too many of those, we are going to get weak, and it does not matter how strong we think we are. From this point on, we need to readjust Who our favor comes from, and Why favor is coming, putting our integrity out front, because a GOOD NAME IS CHOSEN! Nothing can compare to God's love, grace, and mercy, especially when your faith is all you have left.

Life is designed to accomplish a common goal, and that is to serve you. In order for life to serve you, you must know precisely what you want, how you want it, when you want it, and how to PRAY for it! God broke the mold when He created you; but, He has also set certain laws in motion to ensure that you are able to create a mold to manifest the desires of your heart; and, you cannot allow EMOTIONAL FAVORITISM to get in the way, because player hating or hurting the innocent will get you nowhere on this journey!

God does not want us always to react to afflictions, but He wants us to think through it, PRAY about it, and not give up our POWER every time we go through something. The scar may never leave, but that scar could be a representation of where we came from and where we never want to go back to. So wipe those tears away, learn from the experience, get your POWER back and let's hit the training ground with this in mind, *"No eye has seen, no ear has heard, and no mind has imagined what God has prepared for those who love Him"* 1 Corinthians 2:9.

Life may not be fair, but it does offer you a special gift called FAVOR. As the Children of Israel found favor with the Egyptians, they gave them gold, silver, and clothing as they exited Egypt. So shall we find favor as well—this is God's way of blessing us after our trials.

As life presents itself in many different facets, things may or may not go the way you have desired. It's possible that you may win, or you may lose at times, but with divine favor, you will lose to win and win to lose. This is the cycle of life that produces the pruning process that will eliminate the things that are not conducive to you or your well-being. As you very well know, favor may not be fair, but it does take care of the individuals who believe that they are covered with favor. If you have not noticed, favor will always prevail and work in the lives of those who make it their business to do the right thing. Opportunity and favor go hand in hand—if you want favor, embrace opportunity and if you want opportunity, embrace favor. By embracing this concept, you will be able to prosper in any given situation or circumstance regardless of the odds. Hint, hint, a tremendous amount of favor comes when you are able to take the negativity in your life and turn it into something positive.

Regardless of how much you know or don't know, life is designed to give you back what you put into it. Most often, we spend many years finding fault in ourselves, when we should be spending our time enjoying a purposeful life. In order to be more, see more, do more, and have more, you must understand that you are blessed to do what you do!

CHAPTER 5

Training Ground Secrets

As I take you on a journey through Exodus, God will uproot, train, and test you to ensure that you are ready for the next level. This will be accomplished by creating balance that entails changing, transforming old patterns or habits to create new ones, and perfecting our ability to pray. In doing so, you will gain great spiritual insight as well as the knowledge in relation to how your afflicted areas can become your greatest strengths.

Egypt was designed to be the training ground for the Israelites. God was really providing them with the opportunity to gain the skills that they did not possess before coming to Egypt. As a matter of fact, they became excellent in building—building is one tool that God uses to mold His people. With that being said, we all have weaknesses and limitations that need to be reconstructed; and it is through our afflictions that we become great builders as well. We are all born into bondage with an inner born desire to receive our own individual promise; and, for that reason, we all will go through our own Egypt. This is indeed God's way of molding us to think, believe, pray, and do at the same time. In today's world, it's called MULTI-TASKING.

Our life will definitely start taking shape when we provide the mold for it. We all have the option to better ourselves or destroy ourselves by the choices we knowingly or unknowingly make on a moment-by-moment basis. As you very well know, a mold is the framework that produces an end result of what we desire. Not only that, the molding process has a certain order, a certain pattern, or a certain flow that's very distinctive in its characteristics. The only way to obtain order out of a mold is to know the end result of what we want to achieve; which is usually called an OBJECTIVE. Once this is established, then we are better able to set specific goals regarding what we need to do to make our mold complete, what we need to do to receive the finished product, how to develop a timeline for completion, or what we need to pray for. Most often, things fall apart because we do; plus, when we do not put things in the proper PERSPECTIVE, it is extremely hard for our instincts and our conscience to work hand-in-hand, which are desperately needed to ensure that things flow into its proper place.

As we reflect back to the Children of Israel, they built temples and monuments for the Egyptians during their time of enslavement. Even though they were slaves, and their enslavement seemed harsh; but, in my opinion, they were being taught an invaluable skill on how to build, when to build, where to build, and why they needed to pray. Let me explain, the Children of Israel previously lived in the desert; they also lived in tents, which meant that they did not have any former experience in building anything other than tents and   alters. In so many words, they were experienced in setting up things with little or no stability; therefore, their mind was conditioned to that sort of environment. Have you ever put up at tent? It takes little or no skills; even a child can do that. Then, building an altar— it's like building a barbecue pit, come on! Let's compare; they went from building tents to building buildings; come on, apples and oranges. Okay—I'm back on track, you get the picture.

Today we are following the same pattern; we build our lives like a tent, expecting it to endure the trials and tribulations of real life. And, when the issues of life sweep us off our feet and lands us right on our face, then who do we call? We call on God? Yes. That's when we want to pray? That's when we want Him to break His neck for us? However, I encourage praying in our time of need, but don't wait for that moment to pray—it is best to get our brownie points in early in the game by "PAYING IT FORWARD." He has also empowered us with the ability to help ourselves; we must prepare ourselves for life in advance. The storms will come, that's called the CYCLE OF LIFE—you have to suit up, or get swept out! It is not a matter of if a storm will come; it's a matter of WHEN! Having a Tent Life will not sustain a Storm, Hurricane, Tornado, etc. If you follow my lead, I promise you that I am going to give you a few Secrets of Wisdom that will last you a lifetime. Plus, I will show you how to take a tent building mentality of your old mindset, and transform it into a strategic empire building one with a new mindset.

As we move on through this journey, setting up permanent residence in something or someone that's designed to be temporary is one of the quickest ways to find ourselves settling where we don't belong. If something or someone leaves, we must trust life; and we cannot lose our POWER over it, regardless of how bad it hurts. Simply, Pray about it, Grieve briefly, Let go, and Move on. We cannot waste time on something or someone where we are a convenience, and not a priority! Empire building mentalities are never a Mentality of Convenience—we are a Mentality of Priority. Our mind is a mind of VALUE! Where there is lack of value, there will be the lack of priority; therefore, people, places, and things will not be placed in its proper perspective, creating disorder in our lives! Trust me; that SECRET should last you a Lifetime. For that reason, I am here to serve notice that it's time for us to learn valuable skills from those who know what they are doing; therefore, ensuring that we are able to build a life of stability to endure the test of time.

When we have an inner born desire to do something great in our lives, the thoughts of doing so and not doing, will begin to drive us insane! In so many words, it's like having a dream in our heart; and not working toward that dream will deplete our energy just thinking about it. So, why do we waste time thinking about it, when we can spend that same amount of time doing something about it? I'll tell you why, the lack of guidance will often deceive you into feeling as if you are damaged goods. When you are broken with a need for correction, repairing, reshaping, or instructions, who do you go to? Do you go to a doctor, lawyer, friend, husband, wife, or children? Could that be the problem? You are the only one that can answer that question, but I can tell you that the Book of Exodus will probably have the answers or the information that you are looking for; although, they are hidden in plain sight, they are indeed there. As you continue on through this journey, it will be up to you whether you are going to squander your dreams, hopes, and desires or prosper in it. Trust me, your sanity depends on it!

CHAPTER 6

The Playing Field Secrets

The Children of Israel were enslaved for approximately 430 years, according to Exodus 12:40. Can you imagine being a puppet, held back from success for 430 years? Let's be more realistic, what about 40 years? 20 years? 10 years? Or, even 5 years? A person without any idea regarding his or her life is open gain for someone, or anyone to pull their stings by mentally enslaving them.

I know that we all have felt out of control, or as if someone else is pulling our strings. However, being out of control for too long will cause a person's emotions to run rampant. How do you get your life under control? Simply find out what controls you. In so many words, find out what or who is pulling your strings. Once you pinpoint it, take it to God in prayer, while detaching yourself mentally, and then emotionally; and trust me, your body will soon follow! If you are not sure how to do that, simply prevent yourself from reacting in any way, shape, or form, while assuming full responsibility for your role in the situation, circumstance, or event. Remember, positive action will deflate negative action any day. When you get rid of the emotions, your hard work, enthusiasm, and dedication will eventually pay off. As of today, no more excuses for worrying, fretting, fussing, or fighting. So, get the flesh out of the way because this is the first day of your deliverance from bondage.

When God places a calling on your life, from my own personal experiences, it is better to answer the calling or work toward the calling instead of running away. God's plan for your life may be different from what you anticipate. For that reason, Satan may try to block you; but, if you persist, while keeping yourself prayed up, God will clear the way. Or, He may leave a Trail of Nuggets for you to find your way so that His purpose in your life will be fulfilled. Finding the purpose for your life may be unseen for some time, but this is where your perseverance steps in. Basically, your purpose is a mission, vision, calling, passion, or desire, which describes the human need to identify, and express uniqueness. Ultimately, finding your purpose is a spiritual quest, representing your ability to connect with something greater than yourself. Your purpose in life is divinely ordained, as this will become the foundation in which you will continue to build upon for the rest of your life.

If you are becoming a little on-edge regarding your goals in your family life, in your finances, in your marriage, with your education, etc.—it is possible that life is trying to tell you something. As discontentment and boredom set in, you will find yourself searching for people, places, and things to provide a temporary fix to your inner dilemma;

only to find that you are more bored, tired, or disgusted than ever. This is also an indication that you may be experiencing the nudge of or the longing for true success from within, or you are lacking in your prayer life. Basically, this is a burning desire that cannot be put out, a hunger that cannot be fed, or a thirst that cannot be quenched. If you are feeling this way, you are on the right path, keep reading. When designing the life that you want, you must:

- Define and begin to realize who you are right now.
- Understand your strengths and weaknesses.
- Understand what needs to be done to get you where you need to be.
- Understand what skills, education, and experiences are needed.
- Understand God's will for your life.
- Know and understand your passion or burning desire from within.
- Have unwavering faith.
- Know and understand the value of prayer.

The empire that you so desire must be built in your mind before it makes its way to reality. As you very well know, everything you have or do will be formed as a thought, first. Your empire will not come to you by luck; it will come to you by SKILL. Sharpen your mental skills because what you invest in your mind cannot be taken away from you unless you give it away. As you renew your mind on a daily basis, your best bet will be to add in the Word of God, prayer, and meditation to keep the cobwebs of life from blocking your vision.

Satisfaction and fulfillment come from the inside out, not the other way around. Not only that, make sure that you do everything in the Spirit of EXCELLENCE and whatever you want, and/or desire will work, if you work it! Every day gives you an opportunity to become more creative, loving, resourceful, and free. I cannot guarantee that you will become famous or become recognized by the world, but I can guarantee that if you use your talent and/or the gift that's inside of you, you will experience a freedom that you have never felt before. Stay motivated and surround yourself with positive people who believe in you. God is the source that provides the resources needed for the vision that He has placed within your heart. Therefore, you must level the playing field by:

1. Taking a look at your weak spots or your handicaps and make them your best assets instead of weaknesses. Remember, there is something positive in every situation, it's up to you to create a win-win situation by creating **vujá dé**, where you shift your perspective!

2. Finding out what produces outstanding results for you. You don't have to understand it, in order to use it—everything will work itself out.

3. Knowing if you can use it to benefit the lives of others.

4. Knowing if it's worth taking the time to triumph over your tragedy.

5. Knowing if you are willing to make a sacrifice for

it—whatever that "IT" is.

Now, as you prepare for your destiny, focus on the little things you take for granted. Most often, your blessing will be right under your nose—wrapped in a small package.

CHAPTER 7

The Diamond in the Ruff Secret

As we begin to uncover our uniqueness in our lives, it will allow us to build, destroy, or pick up debris. Most often, we will not understand some of the choices that we have made until after the fact. For that reason, my goal is to bring about an awareness of how much power we possess, to ensure that we are able to recognize our behavior in advance as a preventative method to safeguard our future. So let me explain, what we possess from within will allow us to:

1. Build people, places, and things.
2. Destroy people, places, and things.
3. Pick up debris, causing us to become a victim of circumstance.

We are all blessed with specific talents or gifts; they are like diamonds hidden within us. The reason I compare our talent, purpose, or passion with a diamond is because we are not able to see the true value of a diamond until it's cleaned, put through the fire and polished up. This is what I call the extracting and converting technique. Extracting and converting is a hidden technique that is used in bringing forth the buried manifestations of our heart. We use this technique daily without even realizing it. Okay, I will explain what I am talking about. Extracting is basically pulling something out, converting it, and making it into something else.

In order to get to the true diamond in your life, you are going to have to learn how to use this extracting and converting technique. In so many words, you must learn how to extract the positive out of something that doesn't look so great. I must admit, it is going to take discipline, direction, prayer, and determination to master this extracting and converting technique. Bear in mind that you must not allow any situation or circumstance to take you mentally, physically, emotionally, or spiritually to a place that you do not wish to be. It will deplete your Power, affecting your ability to extract, convert, and pray effectively. BEWARE. In doing so, this will give you the incentive to get what you want (positively) without sacrificing your soul or violating your own conscience to get it!

It does not matter whether you are already a diamond or a diamond in the ruff—just keep working toward positively enhancing the lives of others and praying. And, when you can do that, I promise you that the treasure that's hidden inside of you will be revealed. I am a living testimony. I will tell you a true story how I know a diamond can be hidden in the ruff. My late father, Leonard Tolbert, became very ill in my early college years; although I was his only child, I was determined to succeed my own way. He still wanted the best for me, as any father would want for his child. We were from a small country town named Apopka, Florida; His sister, Bessie Vaughn from Opelika, Alabama convinced him that she wanted to see him because she had not seen him in so long. He thought that it was a good idea because he knew that he was very sick, and that he did not have long to live because he was an alcoholic. Before he made his journey to Alabama, he called me into the room and explained to me that he felt in his heart that he did not have long to live. And, that he had worked his whole life to provide enough money for me to survive until I finished college. He said that he was providing a small house so that I would have a place to stay until I finished school to make up for all the years that he abandoned me during my childhood. On that day, I had to promise that I would never drink or smoke as long as I lived. I made him that promise, and I have kept that promise.

He said that it has taken him to face death to realize the value of his only child that he has taken for granted. This was one way for him to right a wrong—the least he could do is to educate me. If he had a chance to change the way he abandoned me, he would; but, what's done is done. He also said that I was very intelligent beyond what he could have ever imagined; and, the least he could do before he takes his last breath is to make a contribution to the wealth of knowledge that I have, because God has truly blessed his child. He said that he was not a rich man; but he has placed his sister Bessie over the money to make sure that I finished college, and she would make sure the bills were paid for me once he passed on. Therefore, I had nothing to worry about, because he knew that my mom was not going to do that for me, she had her own husband to take care of, and he did not want her spending my money on him. So, he went ahead and took care of that in advance to prevent the hassle she would put me through. Once I finished college, he said that I would be able to survive on my own and take care of myself. He then showed me the Certificate of Deposit, and where all of the important documents were, just in case something happened. Did my dad have a feeling about something? He had all of the "Just In Case" planned out, because he knew that if he left me, I would be alone in this world, even though I have a mother!

As my father made his journey to Alabama to visit his sister, he was so happy. He had not seen his sister in a long time, and he could not stop bragging about me. Actually, Leonard Tolbert and his prize child, was the only topic that he would entertain. I am sure he was making a lot of enemies by doing that; but, my dad did not seem to care. He said that he had hidden me for so long that he wanted the whole world to know before he kicked the bucket. I don't know if my dad was making friends or enemies for me; but, sometimes a proud father can make it really bad for a child.

All of a sudden, my ailing father became really, really sick and had to be rushed to the East Alabama Medical Center where he remained for quite some time. I immediately rushed there to visit him; and to their surprise, I was everything my dad was bragging about—he was proud of his child, as every parent should be. The family was really nice, cordial, and very helpful—I had no reason to distrust them.

After going in and out of the hospital over a period of two and a half months, my father finally died. My Aunt Bessie and her niece Barbara Thomas said that they would take care of everything, and I had no reason to distrust that. My father had already discussed with me what would happen—I had no reason to second-guess anything, because I was considered a child, now being overseen by my Aunt Bessie. However, my cousin called warning me to beware; she would not tell me what was going on. My guard went up immediately, as people began to ask for my dad's paperwork, which I did not release.

I had to grow up in a matter of days, as I journeyed back to Alabama with my paperwork, Certificate of Deposit, etc. in hand. As God would have it, as soon as I made it to the State of Alabama—just in time, I walked in the Bank, I saw my Aunt Bessie waiting to cash my Certificate of Deposit. By the Grace of God, if I was a few minutes behind schedule she would have made away with my entire college fund. I know my dad never thought that his sister would do that to his child. I stopped her from cashing the Certificate of Deposit, and I immediately went and got an Attorney, James Sprayberry to represent me. She was no longer an aunt; she was an enemy—she was now after my future.

While my dad was there, Bessie and Barbara had forged a Will taking everything from me; and preventing me from receiving anything from his estate. They had the Will so wayward, that if they could not get anything from my father's estate that it would go to the State of Alabama. No Joke. And, my dad was a Floridian. The Opelika Probate Court allowed them to get away with this forgery. The Will was Prepared and Notarized by Wesley Schuessler, in Auburn, Alabama on December 20 without my knowledge; and my dad passed away on December 26. Their plan was to swindle all of my dad's assets from me; however, Thomas E. Melton represented her. And, since I was his only child, I did have a leg to stand on.   I was able to get the house in Florida, and only half of the Certificate of Deposit. Half of which I paid in legal fees and the other half in the other debts that I accrued in expenses—so, what did I end up with? You got it, NOTHING! Bessie got my father's truck that was registered in the State of Florida; she took it back to Alabama and gave it to her son, David Vaughn. The money my dad left me, she took care of her son with.   Barbara took the rest of the money in the other bank accounts. They took everything else; I could not believe that this was happening before my very eyes—they were like vultures. What could I do, I was still a kid! I was fresh meat, I did not have a clue about life, I am thrown out to the wolves—I really did not know people existed in the world as such.

I did not realize people could take a child's last lifeline—I went back to school struggling, I had nothing. I was literally starving in school—I went for days without eating, I know my dad would have never wanted that for me. It's amazing what people would do to your children when you are not around—I hope that you are picking up some real power nuggets from this story as well. However, the Favor of God was indeed with me, during the summer break I found a pretty good job, and I never made it back to college, vowing to educate myself. I took control of my life, and I have not stopped learning since, I am indeed self-taught. That's why I do not believe in excuses; I believe in taking the bull by the horns and bringing him down by any STRATEGY necessary!

It has not been an easy road, but had it not been for that incident; I would have been a spoiled brat. I would not have

Chapter 7 | Ruby Fleurcius

learned how to work around or how to work through my limits or disabilities. It is for that reason; I do not mistreat people, "That is someone's child that I am mistreating if I do, and I would not be any better than Bessie or Barbara."

Regardless of how anyone tries to paint a picture of me to taint my image, I do not worry at all, because my heart knows the TRUTH. I make it my business to exercise kindness to all—although, I am a stern woman, I am kind indeed. It is having that frame of mind that has polished me into the woman that I am today. I take nothing for granted; but, I was not going to allow Bessie or Barbara to stop me from reaching my goals. I kept moving. I am sure my father is proud of me—I will inspire lives until the end of time with this story, because when you are destined for greatness, nobody can stop it, but YOU. Keep it moving. Whatever you have, it's inside of you. They thought that it was at the University of Central Florida, they thought that it was in that Certificate of Deposit, they thought that it was in the Will that they forged, they thought that it was in my Father's money they took out of the bank, they thought that it was in his truck they gave away, they thought that it was in the house—nope, they missed it! What God had for me, was within me all the time—I just had to see it! That was the turning point in my life. That's where I learned my concept, "Business is Business." What a way to get to the diamond! I must agree—it is shining pretty Bright.

A good ole country THANK YOU to Bessie and Barbara—I was going in the WRONG DIRECTION anyway! My goal was to become an Attorney, and after this happened to me, I made a decision that I would never put a child through what I had to go through. I get questioned quite often, why am I not an attorney; but, I would never tell them the real reason why. However, I am now sharing the reason with the world why Ruby Fleurcius chose to become an Author and not an Attorney at Law. I believe in justice with all my heart, but the justice of man has not proven to be the correct way for me. I chose God instead. The Justice of God, along with the Power of Prayer has worked for me; and I am at Peace with my decision of bringing forth healing, restoration, love, and hope. Through my testimony, I am now creating a WIN-WIN situation for others to learn from. Just in case you miss all of the extracting and converting techniques, I will make it easy for you:

Extracting and Converting Technique:

- Exercise integrity in all that you do. Bessie and Barbara were trying to hurt me, but they really blessed me. I was able to choose the right direction, becoming an Attorney at Law was not my calling. I was called to become a Writer.

- Never mistreat anyone! You never know who or what that child may become. Do you actually think that Bessie or Barbara thought that I would become a Writer? Absolutely not.

- Bragging about your children sparks secret revenge in the family. My father's family plotted secret revenge because they wanted the little money that he had when he died, because he bragged about his daughter too much. When you are not around, some family members will make your children suffer if they feel inferior. Therefore, when bragging about your children, exercise wisdom when doing so, or find people that will celebrate your children with you with no strings or revenge attached.

- Make sure you properly prepare all of your documents for your children with an attorney and through the courts personally, weeding through all the fine print. Do not depend on a family member to do that for you—if you are willing and able-bodied, secure your family assets yourself. Make sure you have backup document—documents get destroyed in the court system. Do not just have one copy! Keep up with your dates, and document often while keeping your children in the loop. There is no figuring it out when you are gone, figure it out now.

- Prepare your children in advance on what to do if something happens. A "To-do" List works well. Train them well—they are never too young. Life happens—don't ever think that money will not change your family members. Had my father not told me what to do, I would not have made it to the Bank in time to prevent my Aunt from cashing my Certificate of Deposit. Therefore, I firmly believe emergency lists are excellent, and every family should have one, especially if you want to preserve your legacy. Our children are our future; you never know who is waiting to take it, or what family member is waiting around to take advantage of your innocent child or children.

- Teach your children how to take care of themselves if you are not around. They need to know how to pray, pay bills, balance a checking account, save money, etc. They are never too young to start learning—if they can zoom through a cell phone like it's nothing, they are old enough to start learning. I had to learn how to do everything on my own. I know that it sounds naive, but I never paid bills until I was on my own—with no training. I had to learn everything as I went along in life, learning how to manage money, etc. In my opinion, a child needs to learn how to manage money at a young age, to ensure that they do not become overwhelmed with debt.

- Learn how to develop a backup plan to make it happen. Teach your children how to exhaust all of their resources before giving up. I was a little country girl that knew nothing but school back then, and I was thrown out to the wolves. I was no match for the grown women, with many years of street knowledge.

- Keep your children in the loop with what's going on—had my father not informed me, I would have been in big trouble with my family.

- Teach your children how to check for unclaimed property that belongs to them. Everyone needs to check periodically for unclaimed monies that go back to the State that we know nothing about. Unclaimed utility deposits, insurance policy payouts, bank account refunds, safety deposit boxes, gift certificates, tax refunds, etc. go unclaimed by the owner or their heirs. Do not pay anyone to do this for you—do it yourself; it is FREE! If it's there, it's your money; you do not have to pay anyone to get it. Go to my website at www.RubyFleurcius.com. Click Unclaimed Money link. Always check at least twice a year for everyone in your family, to ensure that the State is not holding funds that are rightly due to you.

Now, that is some good information for you, not bad for an extracting and converting technique!

CHAPTER 8

The Secrets of Brokenness

In Exodus, Pharaoh's ultimate goal was to kill the Children of Israel's dream—he feared that the Israelites would one day outnumber him, causing rebellion in the land. In order to do so, he had to find a way to destroy the growth process. So, he designed a scheme to kill all the male babies to afflict and stunt the growth of the Israelites. Back then, Pharaoh was the dream killer of the Israelites; believe it or not, his personality traits are still running rampant among us. Actually, he was proud to kill the dreams of the Children of Israel for the benefit of free labor, which is what we often deal with in today's time. How often do we use people to get what we want for free? We do it all the time—there is nothing wrong with helping each other, but there is something wrong with using people or killing the dreams of those who desire more from life. Even though the Children of Israel were oppressed for quite some time, God had a different plan that Pharaoh did not agree with. Of course, we are not all going to agree with the plan of God, but when we fight against God, violating the will of others—then that's a whole different ballgame. God, will shake down heaven and earth to take care of those who pray to Him, trust in Him, and walk in the promises.

Pharaoh's hard heart created a disaster that could have been avoided. Actually, he contributed to his own pain; he contributed to his own downfall, and he contributed to everything that he endured at that time. He made a choice to harden his heart to the will of God. As a matter of fact, this is nothing new, just as Pharaoh fought against the will of God, we do the same as well. Just look around you, do you see destruction or do you see prosperity? A hard heart can and will kill your dreams and the dreams of others if you do not get a grip on it right now. As God works through the hardness that's in your heart, He will help you find value in your valley if you are willing to trust and believe in Him.

Value in the Valley
The broken pieces of your life are nothing more than a shattered vision that needs clearing up. When a person's vision becomes fuzzy or out of focus, there is unresolved or hidden brokenness from within that is most often caused by those who thrive off killing the dreams of others. For the most part, this is not bad if the appropriate adjustments are made in a timely manner. However, as long as you don't throw the pieces of your life away—there is always HOPE! Actually, hope is the glue that gives your broken dreams the ability to bring itself back together again. When you put hope, vision,

prayer, and focus together, it makes a powerful combination that will cause your blessings to chase you down. I will let you in on a little secret, if you want to possess supernatural favor, take the broken pieces of your life, find the positive, focus on what you need to do or what you are not doing, and encourage someone else. If you do this, it will help clear up your dream to ensure that you start reaping the benefits of your brokenness. Trust me—brokenness will have to compensate you for taking up your time!

The higher you value yourself, the better you will feel about you. No matter what you are going through or where you are in life, never deny your worth! The value that you place upon yourself is the price that everyone will have to respect; unless you start giving discounts putting yourself on a bargaining table to be disrespected. "Enough is enough." Stop crying over people that are not crying over you! Stop worrying about situations and circumstances that are not going to change! STOP IT!!!!!! Yes, it is easier said than done but it is also a choice. There is no justifiable reason for you to treat yourself as if you don't matter, or allow others to treat you that way. Just remember, standing up for yourself does not mean that you have to become confrontational or disrespectful. Simply start loving you for you; showing value, honor, and respect for yourself, and others will do likewise.

You will be amazed at what you can do when you don't force grooves to fit where they don't belong. Believe it or not, everything has a place. Now, that you are understanding the importance of prayer in your life, anything that's out of place or does not fit in your life will start making you uncomfortable. As seasons change, some of the grooves in your life will become ajar, creating an imbalance to push you out of your comfort zone or push you into your prayer closet. When grooves fit properly, they create a sense of harmony in your life that's evident in the way you think, speak, move, and handle situations. You will be amazed at what you can do and the goals you can accomplish when you are in the right groove. Simply step outside of your comfort zone to do what you know you can, and do some of the things that you think that you can't do—you never know, you may find the right groove. However, when doing so, please respect and understand the differences of others. Oh, by the way, if you really want your groove back—CHOOSE IT!

Now my question is, "What are you waiting for?" The right time? The money? Someone to help you? STOP WAITING! For every problem, there is a solution. Most often, the solution is deep inside of you. When you feel as if you are at the end of your rope, and the feeling of hopelessness is knocking at your door, just open your heart to divine understanding. It's possible that a vital lesson is not being learned, and this is the time to start seeking for answers. If you make a few mistakes along the way—feel the guilt, forgive yourself, learn from it, and move on because there is always a way out. Just remember, all the answers lie within you. Take one day at a time and take nothing for granted—tomorrow is not promised to anyone; however, you can prepare for tomorrow without compromising the accomplishments you achieve today.

Compromise has often provided temporary comfort to those who are in need of something desperately. Desperate people often do desperate things—it will cause an individual to compromise more than they would care to talk about. As a matter of fact, they would rather keep their hidden acts of compromise in the closet. But that's okay; some things need to remain hidden in the closet, as long as they know and understand the reason for their desperation. Is compromising our integrity really worth it? The answer is NO; however, it can teach us a valuable lesson on how important it is to give in to the passion that's inside of us, rather than to compromise who we are. People may laugh, talk about you or even criticize you, but you must not surrender to the tricks of the enemy or allow them to kill your dream.

The unrecognizable influence of others will prevent you from following the desires of your heart. Please, don't misunderstand me, not all influences are bad; there will always be positive, negative, and neutral influences—the problem comes into play when you cannot recognize the type of influence in your life. Unrecognizable influences are the primary cause of low self-esteem. Individuals with little or no self-esteem feel as if they are not important, and allow others to treat them as if they are not important as well. They often place the needs and feelings of others before their own, eventually causing them to become a people pleaser. A life that is dictated by the thoughts of others will hinder your ability to feel and experience real happiness. A dictated life is not a life that is truly happy. When you become preoccupied with the thoughts of others, you have less time to focus on the things that are truly important to you.

If you haven't noticed, people will treat you exactly how

they see you, and not to mention—you will treat yourself exactly how you see yourself. And, if you neglect you, then you will find yourself in the "Why me?" stage of life. Now, my question to you is, "Why not you?" "If not you, then who?" Who will serve you better than you? Stop acting as if you are the victim—you are no longer a victim of circumstance; you are a victor. You are free; you are no longer in bondage.

For this journey, you must have one heart and one mind. You cannot always determine how people, events, circumstances, and situations enter your life; but most often, you can determine how they leave—positively or negatively. However, you do have control over how people, events, circumstances, and situations affect you. Most often, this is where your inner strength is tested, because self-control is usually one of the hardest things to do. I found that the best way to reap blessings was to leave people, events, circumstances and situations better off than when they entered your life.

I know you have heard it before that happiness is basically a choice. There is no need to try to figure out what's going to make you happy or who's going to make you happy—just BE HAPPY! This will enable the things you want and desire to flow to you naturally. For the record, no more restrictions or conditions on your happiness; for example, "I will be happy when _____" or "_____will make me happy." It's imperative that you must be happy in the NOW, or it will not have lasting value later when you get what you want.

As you move toward your Inner Wealth, there will never be a guarantee that the people around you would recognize the creativity that's inside of you. This is more of a reason to become satisfied from within about the creative lifestyle that you are getting prepared to lead. And, anyone who does not believe in you, is not worth getting upset over. If need be, just allow the criticism of your dream-killers to enhance your determination to get to your promise—your past experiences are over and done with. Furthermore, you don't need people that doubt you in your life anyway—ignore them! Your journey into the Promised Land is too important to allow anyone to get in your way. Focus on the goal and stop wasting time having a pity party, the time clock is still ticking, and it's not going to wait on you. So, get with the program and let's get moving! Keep the image of the promise in your head and consider it done. And let no one take that image from you—no matter what.

CHAPTER 9

The Secrets of Get Out Of Your Way

When we get in our own way, it usually disguises itself as SELF-SABOTAGE. It is so amazing how fear immobilizes your mind and prepares you to create failure by your own actions, where you subconsciously set yourself up for failure based on previous experiences. Fear is a destructive and crippling emotion that will rob you mentally, physically, emotionally and spiritually; therefore, causing you to unawaringly destroy YOU! Fear is created in the mind of an individual and is primarily triggered by low-esteem that appears as fear of failure, fear of being ridiculed, fear of rejection, fear of imperfections, fear of making mistakes, fear of loving again, fear of success, lack of faith, or insecurities with your capabilities, which are created within oneself. With that being said, the more you fear, the more you become a product of fear; eventually, making you self-centered, insecure, unforgiving, tense, miserable and weak; however, fear has only as much power as you give it. If you do not accept fear into your conscious mind, it will not have any power over you—the most amazing **secret** about your mind is that it cannot hold fear and faith at the same time. Now, in order to overcome the barrier of fear, you must be willing to admit your fears, pray about it, and expose yourself to the very things you fear, which means feel the fear of whatever it is, and keep moving toward your promise.

Life has a VOICE, and it has a way of telling you everything you need to know as long as you pay attention without justifying or rationalizing. Would you like to know what life is trying to tell you? If the answer is, "Yes." Keep reading! Whenever you feel a sense of confusion, there is some form of known or unknown distractions in your life. Justifying or rationalizing a true distraction can and will block or hinder the communication between you and your conscience; therefore, hindering your ability to pray effectively. Distractions may come and go; and, for that reason, there is no need to over-think issues. True leaders decide, look for, and initiate change by turning the television or radio off to ensure that they are able to hear what life is saying without any outside interferences. Even though distractions may cause you to lose focus or second-guess yourself, just remember never to give up on YOU! Trust me, if you can admit that someone or something is a distraction in your life, you can get rid of it and turn it into something positive, productive and fruitful.

Settling

The Children of Israel settled in Egypt too long, allowing their dreams to go unfulfilled. In so many words, they became too comfortable with life, settling for mediocrity when God was trying to make them a nation. He caused them to become uncomfortable there, and He also allowed life to become hard—hard enough for them to begin to cry out for help and have a true desire to move out of Egypt. As we all know, this happens to us all the time; God allows our dreams to become shattered causing us to cry out to Him, so that He can move us into position.

Shattered dreams can be restored by not settling for a life of mediocrity; they come into your life temporarily to make you and not to break you. As you know, life is full of surprises and there is no reason for you to give up on yourself or the dream that God has planted inside of you. On that note, when people, places, and things do not welcome you or block you, your best bet is to excuse yourself. In so many words, if someone does not want you, excuse yourself. If a place violates your conscience, excuse yourself. If something does not feel right, excuse yourself. It's okay to excuse yourself from situations and circumstances that are not conducive to your well-being. By excusing yourself from a person, place, or thing does not mean that you have to cover up or not deal with the issue at hand, just don't waste precious time confronting a brick wall, when all you have to do is walk around it. Always remember, what's yours, will be and what's not, will not be! So, there is no need to force yourself to be where you are not welcomed to ensure that you do not settle where you do not belong.

The Children of Israel were great in praying; however, they were waiting for everything to be absolutely perfect for them to move beyond their own limitations.

Not only that, God sent them Moses to deliver them out of bondage. Yet, they found fault in him because he had a stutter. They had their mind set on someone being perfect, not realizing that God gave him the perfect training needed to deliver them out of Egypt. Their faultfinding made their exit more difficult than necessary.

The jaws of perfectionism have a way of killing the dream of individuals who refuse to accept their own mistakes or criticizes others for making mistakes. How do you know if you are a perfectionist? Great question! A perfectionist expects everything to be perfect the first time around without trial and error. Not only that, they want their children to be perfect, they want their family to be perfect, they want their mate to be perfect, they want their friends to be perfect, they want their job to be perfect, and the list goes on. They do not realize that every person, circumstance, or situation is subject to error.

Perfectionism is not inherited as most people think; it is developed during childhood. Most often, it is when a person is made to feel stupid, worthless, or inferior when doing their best. The feeling of not being good enough will cause this perfectionist to procrastinate for the fear of making a mistake or doing something wrong, which hinders their ability to learn from others. Perfectionists are usually classified as the work-a-holics, worry-a-holics, and/or stress-a-holics. Just RELAXXXXXXX! Perfection is a matter of opinion, depending on your perception or a person's perception of what you are doing. If you are honestly and wholeheartedly doing your best, then that's all you can do. Worry, stress, and over-working yourself will not help you on this Journey. Now is the time to lay down the Spirit of

Perfection and pick up the Spirit of Excellence to ensure that you don't kill your own dream. When you are doing your best, and someone decides that they want to throw sludge your way, simply duck, and stand back up again. It does not matter what you do in life; someone will have something to say; sometimes it's positive, and sometimes it's negative. Actually, it is great when it's positive; however, it could be devastating when it's negative. I must admit that it is a challenge to accept negative criticism, especially when you have given your best. Nevertheless, with all due respect, you must find a way to succumb to the fact that negativity is their burden to bear and not yours! You cannot change what people say or do; but, you can change the way you react to what people say or do to you. Try not to become angry, frustrated, confused, or defensive; simply, find a way to embrace the positive and discard the negative, even if it is not applicable to you. Just make it your business to focus daily on finding the positive and it will eventually become second nature.

The spoken words of today will determine what tomorrow holds for you; as a matter of fact, our spoken words are a dead giveaway regarding our thoughts or motives. Of course, we will not be able to control everything that happens to us, but we can control how we deal with it, mentally, physically, emotionally, and most of all, verbally. Inner frustrations that are verbalized negatively can and will cause more hostility than necessary. There is no need for disrespect—what you put out will come back in a full circle, positively or negatively, so beware! Respecting others creates a sense of value that will outlast any superficial façade. Your tomorrow is built upon the decisions that you make on a moment-by-moment basis, making it very important not to use your words loosely. Your best bet is to think before you speak; besides, it only takes a fraction of a second. While doing so, allow yourself to diligently acquire wisdom through listening while availing yourself to be a blessing through your spoken words. That is why I want you to listen to yourself, listen to your heart, listen to your mind, listen to your emotions, and listen to your spirit—the outside world will tell you a lot of things based on their perception. Plus, they will plant unwanted seeds in your heart that will have you growing in the wrong direction; but, if you listen to your positive self, it will cut through a lot of the red tape. Just remember, your heart knows all, just ask questions and your heart will tell you as long as you are willing to listen.

As we listen to life, a critic can sometimes teach us great lessons, if we just push beyond our sensitivities to grab hold of the lessons, instead of grudges. We do not always have to agree to learn; however, in order for us to learn, we must refuse to hold a grudge against someone who has a free will to express himself or herself. As we continue this journey, please do not limit who and what we can learn. There are times when our worst critic has a message for us. Yes, some critics break us down, but some critics can unknowingly build us up if we are willing to stand strong and learn. I understand that correction is not always easy; however, correction creates discipline. It is through our discipline that we are able to accept the information from our critics, process what's beneficial and discard the rest.

As a matter of fact, this is where your filtering process comes into play, filtering out the negative and embracing the positive. Hint, hint, your critic may be discreetly challenging you in the areas that you are weak, broken, or torn down. Furthermore, with or without your critics, it is time for you to take charge and go into your promise knowing that all things will work together for the good as long as you do not limit your ability to learn, understand and move on. With that in mind, positive perseverance will produce steadfast characteristics inside of you that will seek to balance out issues that are creating problems in your life.

Excuses

No more excuses, own up to your faults, and you will find peace beyond all understanding. Stop complaining to God, to people, and to yourself—just give thanks. This is the most effective way to mature in the areas of your life that have been forgotten about and neglected. I know there are times when you feel as if God is picking on you, but it is the total opposite—you are being highly favored. Real or imagined obstacles are basically opportunities waiting to avail itself in your life. Obstacles are not meant to break you, even though you may feel broken; they are designed to test you, teach you, prepare you, push you, or motivate you to action. If you want to gain control over your life, you must assume responsibility for your actions, reactions, and decisions—trust me, peace will find you even if it is not your fault!

CHAPTER 10

Secrets of the Plagues

The Children of Israel found it hard to believe that God sent them a deliver until Moses showed them the signs of God. Moses threw down his staff; it became a snake and back again; he also put his hand inside his garment and withdrew his hand covered with leprosy and back again. God sent these signs so that the Children could prepare themselves mentally to accept the miracles, signs, and wonders that were going to take place during and after their journey out of Egypt. Now, before God brought the Children of Israel out of Egypt, He had to put a system in place, which consisted of Moses receiving instructions or prophetic messages directly from Him. Then, Moses relayed the message to his brother Aaron, and then Aaron relayed the message to Pharaoh.

Moses demanded the freedom of the Children, as the scripture states, he told Pharaoh that God commanded for him to let His people go, so that they may go into the wilderness to make a sacrifice. Of course, Moses was not going to tell Pharaoh about the Promised Land—Moses knew that Pharaoh's goal was to play the power card with him. This power play actually became the battle of the gods—little gods against God Almighty. God had a plan for their exile, and He has a plan thousands of years later for your exile as well. In today's reality, God will not speak to your Pharaoh; He will speak to you, and you must then be willing to get your thoughts together and speak to your own Pharaoh—He may or may not use a third party in dealing with the Pharaoh that's in your life. What is our Pharaoh? Everyone's Pharaoh will not be the same, but our Pharaoh is anything or anyone that's holding us back, keeping us in bondage, or controlling us.

Now, your job is to knock them down, one at a time. If you desire to be released, you must be able to tell your Pharaoh to "let you go." Just remember that your burdens may increase, and your life may seem like it's spiraling out of control; but, that's only your Pharaoh's resistance in letting you go. However, when it's time for your exit, God will put any and all of your little gods to the test. In order to better determine if you have any known or unknown pharaohs in your life, take a look at the plagues of Egypt. The plagues could mean a lot of different things; I am not interpreting the plagues—I am simply bringing them to life.

1. **Blood.** This is a sign of contamination. If you notice, things will stop growing in your life. You may stop growing, or there will be constant failure in your life that blocks your prosperity.

2. **Frogs.** This is a sign of distractions. You will jump from one thing to the next with little or no consistency in what you do or say. This will cause you to lack focus in areas of your life that really need your attention.

3. **Lice.** This is a sign of irritating attachments. This is when people, places, and things will seem as they are attaching themselves to you, causing you to become irritable. This is where the little things will start rubbing you the wrong way.

4. **Flies.** This is a sign of compromise. When things begin to spoil in your life, you must double-check to see where you are compromising your integrity. At this point, when there is compromise, whatever it is will not work, and it will find wings and depart from you anyway. So, is it really worth it? Is greed really worth it? Is selfishness really worth it? Are your possessions really worth it? What would it profit a man to gain the whole world and lose his soul?

5. **Disease.** This is a sign of sickness. This is when the people, places, and things in your life cause you to become sick—mentally, physically, emotionally, or spiritually. This is so prominent now more than ever. When we become too bull-headed, not letting go of things that are not good for us, we will suffer the consequence of some form of sickness.

6. **Boils.** This is a sign when our sickness is exposed to everyone. It is one thing to become sick without anyone knowing about it. But, when your sickness is exposed, it leaves room for judgment as well as public embarrassment.

7. **Hail.** This is a sign of when our hearts become cold and hard. There is nothing worse than having our hearts hard as a rock or cold as ice. This is actually when we become angry at life, angry with people, or just angry about everything. Unjustifiable anger will begin to break down other areas of our lives.

8. **Locust.** This is a sign of a non-profitable harvest. This is when we work all week long and when we get paid, our money finds holes in our pocket. Unexpected bills will begin to pop-up taking all of our extra money—it is sad when we cannot find a way to profit from our labor.

9. **Darkness.** This is a sign of hopelessness. This is where we begin to start giving up. Unexpected darkness decreases our hope to see the light at the end of the tunnel. And at this point, if we don't make the effort to turn the gloomy areas into areas of light, we will then force ourselves into the last plague.

10. **Death.** This is a sign of being at our ultimate low. To suffer a slow death from within is the

worst death to die. Of course, we will not get to this point, because we are going to make our turn-around. And, this is where you are going to have to ask God to Passover you—you are going to have to cover yourself with the Blood of Jesus Christ to protect the nation that resides within you.

Regardless of who or what's your Pharaoh, these plagues serve as a representation of what could happen if you hold on to the little gods of your life. The plagues may or may not affect you personally; it may affect the people, places, and things that are in your environment. Just know that you are not alone, God will go to war for you, preventing the plagues from entering your life, but you must do your part to ensure that you are willing to move out of the familiar into the unfamiliar, while incorporating the Power of Prayer. You have a Nation inside of you waiting to possess its own land.

The Passover

If you have battle with any form of plague in your life—**YOU MUST MAKE PRAYER A PART OF YOUR DAILY REGIMEN.** In order for certain things to PASSOVER you, a commitment to prayer is a must. For example, you would not drive your vehicle without the proper coverage, right? Same principle! Yes, having faith is one thing—faith alone without works will not get us to the place where God would truly desire for us to be. In fact, doing things backward or unequipped will cause us to experience a sense of emptiness or disorganization that is totally unexplainable to the average person. Well, how do you know what you are equipped for? Great question!

Start writing down the things you like and the reasons why. Then ask yourself, "If this had no added benefit, would I still enjoy doing it?" And, "Would it benefit the lives of others?" If the answer is "yes." Then, you must work toward it; I am not saying give up your job, to drop everything, or everybody in your life; but I am saying, work on a plan that's able to fit into your lifestyle without having to go cold-turkey on people, places, and things that are in your life. Just remember that with all things, it takes time and with time comes divine favor if you do not give up on yourself.

This is the point of your new beginning, passing from the things of old into the things of the new—giving you the right to ask the Holy Spirit to dwell within you, to transform and renew you. As *"The Spirit of truth will guide you into all truth" John 16:13,* make it your business not to be consumed by the Pharisee spirit. This is a judgmental spirit that condemns people who are different from you or people who are going through a phase in their life that's not pleasing to you. Love and grace need to be exercised at all times—this does not mean that you allow people to walk all over you or for you not to exercise tough love. It means exercise love and grace in the way you treat others without passing judgment; however, there need to be a constant evaluation of everything that you do. In the evaluation process, you must take into account:

1. Your willingness to face all of your fears.
2. Your willingness to let go of indecisiveness.
3. Your willingness to release all attachments to codependency.

4. Your willingness to listen to your conscience, inner nudges and to life itself.
5. Your willingness of obedience, discipline, and organization.
6. Your willingness to activate your problem-solving skills.

As you allow yourself to become willing, repeat daily; *"My God will supply all I need according to His riches in glory by Christ Jesus." Philippians 4:19.* The Holy Spirit will be the light that guides you to your promise. When the Spirit of the Lord comes upon you, it will be the most empowering experience you will ever encounter. He will guide you through the good and bad times that you will endure on the journey, as the word states clearly, *"Not by might, nor by power, but by My Spirit, says the Lord of hosts." Zechariah 4:6.*

For every problem, there is a solution! Most often, the solution is deep inside of you. You just have to pray about it, put one foot in front of the next, and start walking toward your goal, and let the power within you be your guide to problem-solving one-on-one by:

1. Writing the issue down on paper without judging it.
2. Asking yourself if you're willing to let go of it.
3. Answering the when's, where's, how's, and why's about what you need to let go of.

Common sense is not at all common if you refuse to think inside the box, outside the box, through the box, and around the box. Most often, we tend to focus on thinking outside the box, forgetting that the inside is just as important as the outside. Of course, we all think a little different based on our values, principles, and conditioning. And, what's common sense for one person may or may not be common sense for the next person; making it very, very important to view life from 4 angles:

1. View life in the box **understanding** your limits and boundaries.
2. View life outside the box **expanding** your territory.
3. View life around the box being **open** and **honest** with yourself.
4. View life through the box, lining yourself up with Godly characteristics and principles.

In order to maximize what's on the outside, you must understand what's on the inside and be able to think through the process of doing both. This will ensure that you do not look over pertinent areas of your life that need your attention. The key word here is to THINK. No matter what's going on in your life, you CAN think your way through it until you can think your way out of it. Any issue can be resolved as long as you assume responsibility for your part in it. This journey demands perseverance, sacrifice, a positive attitude, and a lot of effort. If you are always thinking of something better—STOP IT. Enjoy every moment of your life, because if you don't, you will never be satisfied by anyone or anything. Challenges will come, and they will eventually go, as long as you assume the position of making your objectives clear and precise by:

1. Writing your goals down, keeping them where you are able to see them every day.
2. Mapping out your journey.
3. Having an idea of what it's going to take for you to get to your destination?
4. Knowing approximately how long it will take you to get there?
5. Knowing some of the sacrifices?
6. Deciding if you are willing to make those sacrifices?
7. Knowing how your goal will benefit you and the lives of others?

Don't rush the process; it takes time to get to your destination. Rushing will cause you to make unwise decisions that will prolong the process or get you side-tracked. Anything that's little in the beginning will grow if it is fertilized and watered properly; however, let me clear this up, your skills, talents, and abilities are useless if they are not utilized according to the purpose of its intent. Action is the key word here! It is very important to put some action behind your blessings; I must admit, a little may not be enough if you work on whatever it is sporadically. Rest assured that it is not wise to do things only when you feel like it—this will only limit your results. On this journey, whether you feel like it or not, you have to work with the little that you have consistently to increase your productivity. Now the ideal question is, "What skills, talents, and abilities do you possess and have not used?"

Simply make a list of them, and make a commitment to work on them every day.

Down and Out

When you are down and out, you must keep your head up to ensure that you don't get stepped on and kicked around. When a person gives up on life—it shows. It shows in their face, in their attitude, in their reaction, in the way they treat others, and so on. For someone that has given up, it causes them to become a victim—victim of circumstance and a professional victim of life.

Everyone will have peaks and valleys in their lives; however, your ability to climb out of the valley will determine your ability to rise to the top. There may be times when you feel as if you can't get out of whatever you are in; yet, that is your moment to look up and trust God. Your life is not over. It is possible for you to be on the brink of losing your mind before you actually make a conscious decision to change your mind. Everyone is going to go through something, whether they want to or not. There are times when we will have to start losing something to realize the true value of it. And, just because a person has a few negative challenges in their life does not mean that they have to continue to stay challenged. As a matter of fact, it is through the tough times in life that causes an individual to fight for their sanity.

Your thoughts will eventually create your known or unknown reality. Take a moment to regain your thoughts to ensure that you keep them positive, productive, and fruitful; furthermore, your experience in life is totally up to YOU. Don't waste time being resentful over your past experiences, pick up the pieces and move on with your life. This will ensure that you don't allow the negative to deprive you of your opportunity to live a positive, balanced lifestyle. Just remember, if you come out of something mentally, your body will soon follow. Life gives you the opportunity to plan for your come back as long as you do not give up on yourself. Align your thoughts and actions to represent your predetermined victory. From me to you, once you are at the peak of life, reach down, and pull someone else up out of the valley without judging him or her. Enjoy life and life will enjoy you.

CHAPTER 11

The Impedimental Secret

In Exodus, Moses had a complex about being a man slow of speech. When God spoke to him at the burning bush, the insecurity about his stutter came up not only one time, but several times during his conversation. Eventually, God sent Aaron, his brother, as a mouthpiece. That was God's way of giving him a sense of security—especially, coming from being a prince in Egypt for 40 years, to being a shepherd on the far side of the desert for another 40 years. As I see it, God trained Moses to experience both sides of having much wealth and having so little that feels like a form of slavery. With all of that being said, Moses had to deal with a self-identity crisis that had been brewing for years as he tended flocks of sheep. Moses saw tending sheep as an insignificant job, but God was really teaching him how to become a shepherd over the Children of Israel. This experience really taught him how to become patient as he had no other choice but to talk to sheep all day. Although this may sound insignificant—this was basically his classroom on learning how to guide, teach, and minister to the needs of God's people. God knew that the Children of Israel could not be left alone, so they needed someone to lead the way, set goals, and pray on their behalf. Even though Moses had a stutter, so did the Children of Israel—they just had a different form of stutter that prevented them from hearing the Voice of God. Their stutter was:

1. The Stutter of Complaining.
2. The Stutter of Ungratefulness.
3. The Stutter of Judgment.
4. The Stutter of Self-Control.
5. The Stutter of Slave Mentality.
6. The Stutter of Their Faith.

All of these stutters are impediments that displeased God. The **Secret** is that w e are able to overcome or work through any type of impediment if we learn how to become HUMBLE enough to set goals and work on them. Many individuals don't plan or set goals because they don't know how or they are afraid of their impediment. An impediment is designed to impede upon our goals, creating a distraction preventing us from setting them. Our superficial impediments have cause more false sense of failure than a real handicap itself. Our stutter has become our way of making an excuse for not doing. We tell ourselves that we are not good enough, it will not work, we are wasting our time, or that we cannot accomplish anything. However, in all those excuses, I have found that there are 3 types of people:

1. People who wish things could happen.
2. People who stand around to talk about & criticize what happens.
3. People that have the faith to make things happen and to become effective.

Impediments are designed to drive greatness out of us, regardless of how it may seem at the time. An impediment is basically an obstruction or hindrance that will create a superficial image of weakness. When a weakness is exposed to others, most often, we retreat out of shame instead of taking our weakness and turning it into something great. A weakness exposed is better than a weakness covered up. As a matter of fact, an exposed weakness will give us more of an incentive to work on that area. When our weakness is covered up, it is easier to overlook it, make excuses for it and pretend that it doesn't exist. The truth is, we all have some form of an impediment. Some are able to cover them up better than others, but in all reality, we all fall short in some area of our lives. However, this is not the time to worry about falling short or being perfect; because an impediment cannot keep you blocked if you look for the benefit and plead the Blood of Jesus on it. And, when you do that, greatness is inevitable, creating an open door of opportunity for you to map out your destiny; and, more than likely, that is indeed your **Blessing** in disguise.

A goal is a road map; it will tell you where you are, what you need to do, and how to get there. Those who do not have goals set for themselves, usually wonder aimlessly through life working toward nothing. As a result of working toward nothing, they will soon start settling for things that are not a part of them, not a part of their purpose, and it contradicts everything that they believe in. Consequently, without a goal, plan, or purpose, it will become hard for them to understand and know where they are going. When defining your goal and purpose in life, take whatever time is necessary to study, plan, and think. Put in writing your step-by-step plans and ideas you intend to use to accomplish your goal. In the planning process, you must keep each item separate. Write out your specific goal or purpose in life. After each item, write down why you want to achieve it. Here are a few questions to get you started:

1. What do you value the most?
2. What is your most important goal?
3. If you only had 1 year to live, what would you do?
4. What do you love to do?
5. What makes you feel important?
6. What's the risk?
7. What are the pros and cons?
8. What are the obstacles involved?
9. What will you have to sacrifice in your life?

In order to commit yourself to your goal, you must enter into a binding contract. This will become your contract between you and God. When you continuously embed this burning desire on your subconscious mind, it will become a desire that will consume you until you have achieved it.

Try to be as clear and detailed as you can. Include all of the goals you want to achieve, the knowledge you will need, what occupation you want to engage in, the kind of person you want to become, the income you want to earn, etc. Aim for the gift that is within you; if you do not—you will miss out every time.

There are times when you may have to keep it to yourself, so that you will not put yourself in a position to be talked about, criticized, or discouraged from achieving your goals. I have found that setting goals:

- Help you to stay focused and achieve more.
- Prevent confusion from within.
- Provides more confidence.
- Peace of mind.
- Creates more joy and satisfaction.
- Keeps you motivated to perform at your best.

Get rid of the shoulda, coulda, and woulda syndrome. Use I can, I will, and I expect. Your goals in life will become your treasure map to success. It may not be easy, because if it were easy, everyone would be able to do it. God will not place a desire in your heart that He cannot manifest. After you have signed your commitment, read it out loud at least 7 times each morning and 7 times before going to bed at night for 40 days and once thereafter until your goal is achieved. This will help you get focused on doing what you have to do, to get to where you need to be in life. In order to eliminate backtracking, you must have your road map handy at all times, so that you can make the right turn at the right time. Therefore, mark your destination and allow God to become your tour guide through His Word and by your Faith in Him.

In creating a plan for succeeding with your goals in life, you need to know what it is that you want to believe in. That is why it is very important to plan your success and make it happen by asking yourself 7 integrity finding questions:

1. Can I honestly ask God's help in striving to reach this goal?
2. Will it get me where I want to go?
3. Will it violate God's laws?
4. Will it violate my conscience or override my purpose?
5. Will it violate the rights of others?
6. Will my family be able to enjoy the rewards of my accomplishments?
7. Am I willing to do what it takes in order to succeed?

It is possible that you may have to revise your goal list on a certain day every month. Put the achieve goals on your "Thank God Victory List." Put your major goals on a 3 x 5 card and carry it everywhere you go. When you have to make a big decision, ask yourself:

1. Is it according to the Will of God?
2. Will it get me closer to my goal or purpose?
3. Will it help or hinder me?
4. How do I feel about it? If you feel confused,

disoriented, or have any type of funny feeling, this should be a red flag.

A strong enough passion for something will enhance our sense of direction that will drive us to our goal or away from our goal. Just remember, our sense of direction is often blinded by our inability to recognize our goal setting capabilities. For example, we achieve many goals on a daily basis; such as getting up in the morning, taking care of ourselves, taking care of our family, cooking a meal, driving to our destination, getting to work on time, etc. Yet, we consider ourselves a failure when we do not achieve a goal that has our attention. All goals, big or small, deserve our attention! Think through your goals and do not set them too low, but you also want your goal attainable, and become thankful for the small goals on a daily basis, and those big goals will come.

CHAPTER 12

Secrets Of The Voice From Within

Your instincts will tell you what most people will not, the only requirement that's needed is for you to open up and listen to the voice from within. Once you are open to listening, the voice from within will speak louder than the loudest person you know. Not only that, it will give you a little nudge or a funny, uncomfortable feeling as well. This is basically your senses alerting you to pay close attention to what you are doing, what you are saying, or any decisions that you are about to make. Trust me; an instinctual nudge is something that's more precious than fine gold—this is your **POWERHOUSE**. And, for that reason, no more rash decisions; take your time to think about what you are doing and why you are doing it. Remember, the Holy Spirit is going before you and if there's a battle from within about a situation, circumstance or decision, take your time to find out what's going on from within, FIRST.

There are times when life protects you for a greater known or unknown purpose; and it does not matter whether it is good or bad, positive or negative—life's destructive forces have a way of manipulating you to violate your own conscience. Basically, the destructive and negative forces that are around you are empowered by your thoughts, fears, actions, and reactions. As a matter of fact, when you do things that violate your conscience, it is nothing more than a forewarning of things to come. Your conscience serves as a buffer, signaling you to take a break and reevaluate whatever you are doing, thinking, saying, or wanting. In fact, your restrictions may not be the same as someone else; however, most restrictions are placed where you are the weakest or the most egotistical. Furthermore, a temporary sacrifice of a violated conscience is not worth the permanent pain or scar.

Injustices are a part of life that comes with lessons and blessings to prevent a lifestyle of déjà vu. Who said that life would be easy? Well, it's not easy. Our lives are full of choices day in and day out; some choices that we want to make and some that we don't. Most often, the decisions that we don't want to make are often served to us as an injustice that forces us to make a decision. An injustice (being wronged) comes into your life for two reasons:

1. To let you know, that's NOT your blessing.
2. To cause you to doubt your blessing.

If you can find your way through the wrongness, there is rightness on the other side; but, you must find out what your injustice is trying to tell you. Once you find out, you must prevent yourself from being consumed by negative emotions that will cause history to repeat itself. You have the key to open the door to lessons and blessings that will enhance your life beyond what you could ever imagine. Just remember that true success is not about material gain or throwing your power around; it's about doing what you love and love what you do, and changing your perception about an injustice through what I call **vujá dé**!

The Voice from within, our instincts, and our conscience are all one in the same; but they are also consider to be your natural navigational system that will keep you from wasting time and energy on people, places, and things that are not conducive to your well-being. A very small portion of our population actually uses their natural navigational system, often causing most individuals to have a poor sense of direction. As a matter of fact, when we have a poor sense of direction, we are often bombarded with constant obstacles to keep us distracted from knowing where to go next and what to do. Of course, you will get off track from time to time, but if you allow the **secret** navigational system that God placed inside of you to work for you without resisting it, it will get you back on track every time, even if He has to create a way for you!

CHAPTER 13

The Purification Secret

The Children of Israel finally embarked upon their journey out of Egypt, taking them into the great unknown. However, they did not realize that their journey would become their purification process. Yes, God brought them out of Egypt, but He also had to get Egypt out of them. As they cleaved to a past life that no longer existed, turning back was no longer an option. However, the mere act of dwelling on their past hindered them from embracing the fullness of their movement forward. Once God brought them out of their Egypt—THAT WAS IT! And the same applies to you; this is your exit out—you can say that this is your coming out or your homecoming, whichever way you want to refer to it—you will not be the same once you are done reading this book. God has already provided a map for your journey through the Book of Exodus; therefore, you will be able to define or better understand how your story will really end.

On this journey to your Promised Land, you are going to be faced with obstacles. Someone may be occupying your blessing, and you may suffer some loss; however, you must not run from experience, all you have to do from this point forward is to LEARN. During this time, problems on your job may come up, stand still; your health may decline, stand still; you may have problems in your home, stand still; you may have problems in your relationship, stand still; people may talk about you, stand still; your bills may be behind, stand still; you are gaining weight, stand still; problems in the church, stand still; there is not enough time in the day, stand still and see the Salvation of the Lord. There is no need to complain, fuss, or fight—you are in your wilderness; however, you want to make sure that you are not making the same mistakes that the Children of Israel made.

Challenges will come to make you stronger; but, do not rush the process. It takes time to get to your destination—rushing or becoming impatient will cause you to make unwise decisions that will prolong the process or get you sidetracked. And, without a doubt, a little perseverance, obedience, prayer, and dedication will eventually get you there. Don't be afraid to take the journey; there is a great opportunity waiting for you on the other side of that learning curve. Furthermore, it will take you just as much energy to go back where you came from, as it will to keep going toward your destiny.

As you continue on this journey, it's not going to do you any good to stay in the Word of God 24 hours a day 7 days a week, if you are not willing to become HUMBLE to the leading of the Lord or NEGLECT your prayer life.

Actually, God would much rather for you to "live the word and not know it; than to know the word and not live it." He wants you to be a part of what He is doing and what He's willing to do in your life. Even though you may not understand what's going on, you must find a way to trust and know that He is God—He will clear a path for you, clean up the trash in your life, make a way out of no way, and lay a path to GUIDE YOU. The only requirement is that you continue to place one foot in front of the other without watching, questioning, and doubting every step before you take it. Most often, your success will be based upon your determination to use what you already have inside of you, to enrich the lives of others. Simply look up to your Heavenly Father as you become Spirit Led, allowing Him to guide your every footstep—soon enough, you will be able to watch the chains fall off every area of your life. God will never take you, where He can't keep you.

Shortcuts in life are not always easy or right; sometimes when you try to make something too easy for yourself, you miss out on the most important lessons; therefore, causing you to become a professional victim. These are the types of people that are easily frustrated and constantly driven by things that cause them to become depressed. This does not necessarily make them a bad person; they just need to become more aware of what's causing them to repeat the same cycle over and over. Things may not be easy, but you can definitely make them SIMPLE. Keeping life simple will probably be the easiest way to keep your life on track without compromising or sacrificing your integrity. How do you keep life simple? Great question! Remember, there is a lesson to be learned in everything—learn the lesson, keep it positive, and move on to help and inspire others to do the same. Could it possibly be that easy? Sometimes "yes" and sometimes "no"; but this will keep you from becoming a professional victim of circumstance! Your thoughts, words, and actions influence the direction in which you will take toward your destination. There will be many roads in life—some long, some short, and some will be dead-ends. Nevertheless, whatever road you choose, you must have a destination in mind, or you will wander aimlessly. SO WHAT, if you take the wrong road, that's one road that you cannot travel again. If you ever find yourself on the wrong road or at a dead end—quickly, reevaluate the situation or circumstance, find out where you went wrong and simply, turn around. After today, no more pity parties, no more feeling sorry for yourself, and no more passing the blame. No matter how long it takes for you to get to your destination, keep moving, remain positive, and speak life into your situation, you will get there.

CHAPTER 14

The Reciprocity Secret

As the Children of Israel traveled the desert, God provided everything that they needed for the journey. It was their season to move out of slavery and into a life of freedom. The only seeds that they had to plant on their journey to the Promised Land were seeds of love, faith, prayer, and obedience. However, as soon as something changed or they became challenged in some way, they became angry and rebellious. They did not realize that the same way that God brought them out of Egypt—He could take them into their Promise. Sadly to say, they could not see the forest because they had an illusion of trees standing before them mentally.

Things change around us and within us as the seasons do. The problem with us is that we try to stop the season or make the season come before it's time, defying divine order. God did not intend for anything to stay the same, and that includes you! Stop trying to change everyone else and allow God to change you. Whenever you get into the mentality that everyone else needs to change, that is an automatic sign that you have issues within yourself that need to be worked on. As a matter of fact, people become a little insecure and rebellious when or if you try to change everything about them. Furthermore, you are only fooling yourself if you think you can change someone else without you changing Y.O.U! When you change, then others will change; until then, you are fighting a losing battle.

Growing is one aspect of life but growing properly is another. Most often, we focus on outer growth and forget about the growth that takes place on the inside of us. Unfortunately, if the inner growth is forgotten about, it becomes devastating to the management and accountability of everyday life. In so many words, your life will begin to spiral out of control. It is easier to shift your accountability over to other people, but all this does is cause you to become codependent. Codependency stunts the growth of all who fall into its trap. Yes, it is nice to have people to help you and to do nice things for you. However, when you depend on others to make you happy, eventually it will create problems in your life. In fact, once you become accountable for your own life, the generosity of your own solutions will become inevitable.

Nothing teaches character better than generosity. Nevertheless, with generosity, comes with its twin sibling called reciprocity—they are inseparable twins that serve their own unique purpose. In fact, generosity is the first-born of what you give out positively or negatively and reciprocity is the second-born the holds the leg of its firstborn sibling until its birth order is complete. In so many words, what we give out generously, reciprocity will bring back in full circle in due season, regardless of whether it's positive or negative. We very rarely hear about reciprocity, but it is by far the "GOLDEN RULE" principle of giving and receiving. Of course, it is more than just giving money—it's giving your time, knowledge, wisdom, and most of all, the more familiar adage of, "Do unto others as you would have them to do unto you." Using people to get what you want is the quickest way to lose it. Conniving and scheming to get people to do stuff for you is not the way to get things done. People will naturally help you if you just ask for it. It is okay to ask for help, but the quickest way to receive help is to give it freely.

Giving has much more power and authority than you will ever possess. The more you give, the more life will be able to give back to you. In so many words, what you give out is an investment in your future, which will return to you multiplied many times over. For that reason, you must make sure that you always give out goodness and not evil. Today, find a way to invest into someone's life and someone will eventually invest in you.

The excitement of getting something new will never supersede the Law of Reciprocity. When the newness of something wears off, then what do you do? Throw it to the side, get rid of it, ignore it, or move on to something different? Of course, it really depends on the situation or circumstance that caused the loss of excitement. But, for the most part, there are certain things that you cannot just get rid of without paying a very high price for doing so. Now the question is, "What do you do in a catch-22 situation like this?" The answer is really, really simple—Give! I am going to let you in on a big **secret**—giving overcomes the sense of dissatisfaction. Most often, dissatisfaction is presented in your life when you want things for the wrong reason, but if you GIVE for the right reason, or share some of your **Blessings** with those who are in need, it creates a counteraction. Whatever area of your life that you are feeling a little dissatisfied in, your best bet is to give in that particular area to make a positive difference. How do you know what to give? Again, great question! You have to allow your conscience to guide you in how, when, and what to give, when to give in and what you need to give up. Not only will this enhance your life, but it will also give you a sense of peace that's beyond human understanding. You were born to empower, encourage and enhance the lives of the people that you come in contact with on a daily basis. YOU are the gift that keeps on giving!

CHAPTER 15

The Secrets of "Owning It"

Most often, at some point in our lives, we find it hard to admit that we may have made a mistake.   The keyword here is to ADMIT. Refusing to admit mistakes will contradict or compromise a person's ability to learn, adapt, and adjust to change. As a matter of fact, just because a bad decision is made in climbing up the wrong tree, does not necessarily mean that a wrong decision was made. It is possible to make the right decision to do the wrong thing! In doing so, it will do two things: 1. BREAK YOU.   2. MAKE YOU. In so many words, God will break you out of your old habits or limitations, and put you back together by transforming you into a person of substance. Easier said than done, right? But it is doable! For the simple fact that you never, ever want to bear fruit in the wrong tree; because bearing fruit in the wrong tree, could be devastating if you allow the bad or wrong fruit to take root in your heart. Better yet, start listening and allowing your conscience to become your guide as you wait on God to synchronize your heart and your mind.

Your blessing requires you to have the patience to stand on that mountain that will not move. Now let me ask you, "If your blessing came right now, would you be able to handle it?" Most people would say "yes." A quick "yes" to me, is an automatic "no", you are not ready. Who am I to judge? Absolutely, it's not my place, but I am saying that it takes a little time to evaluate your readiness for your blessing. Think about it; if you were really ready, God would not deprive you of anything good. It takes time for the filtering process to take place and for God to properly bless you. As a rule of thumb, what comes fast goes fast—never rush it, just persist with it. Oh by the way, if you fall off that mountain—just get up, start climbing back to the top again and wait on God.

Patience, faith, and prayer are key players in finding the right solution to any situation or problem. Patience is the ability to endure your pains, stresses, or hardships calmly and without complaint. Now, impatience is the opposite; it is the inability to cope with pains, stresses, and hardships. As a matter of fact, impatience is not of God—I personally know that it is human nature to want an immediate answer in time of heartache and trial. However, in the midst of your trial, do not, and I mean do not rush to make any unwise decisions. Be very cautious, it is Satan's deceptive measures that will try to push you into getting ahead of the Will of God. Meanwhile, God knows what He's doing, and He uses the tool called **TIME** to accomplish His great works.

CHAPTER 16

The Secrets of Your Hand

As Moses led the Children of Israel out of Egypt, they journeyed through the desert, making it to the Red Sea. As you can imagine, it became chaotic—they had the sea in front of them, mountains on both sides of them, and Pharaoh's army behind them. Of course, the Children of Israel had to learn how to stand still, while it seemed as if they were stuck between a rock and a hard place. But, here again, God had a plan. As Moses PRAYED, he was reminded that he had a DIVINE TOOL in his hand. That something of a tool was his rod, as he lifted that rod to our Heavenly Father, the Lord our God divided the waters of the Red Sea. With the amazement of all, the Children of Israel were able to walk on dry land to get to the other side. As the Egyptian Army pursued them, God allowed Moses to use that same tool to cause the waters of the Red Sea to come crashing down—separating them from Egypt, once and for all. You will notice that every miracle that was performed had something to do with what Moses had in his hand. Now, what tools do you have in your hand that can create a Red Sea experience in your life? What gift, talent, or skill can you lift up to God? Or, better yet, what situation, circumstance, event, or issue do you need to lift up to God in prayer?

God can and will divide whatever's chasing us; but, there is a catch. He will not part that sea until we are ready to walk through it with our tool in hand. That **secret** tool is called prayer! This will also put us in a position to become totally dependent upon God; especially, when it seems as if there's nowhere to go. God will take us through those wet places while opening doors that only He can open. And, once we cross this sea, we will never be the same again. This is His way of taking us out of something that we must never walk back through again. Trust me, regardless of what challenges you may endure; the enemy will lose its grip on your life if you never lose your song. When you keep your song in your heart, you will better understand how the rod of correction is necessary to keep us on a straight and narrow path.

The Rod

The Children of Israel were in desperate need of correction, and they did not realize it. Correction is a hard thing to accept, but it is the best weapon used in attracting success. Rules are not made to be broken; they are made so that we would have limitations. Knowing our limitations will keep us sane; as a matter of fact, we all stand to be corrected at some point in our lives, and that is okay! Most often, we do know the difference between right and wrong; but out of selfishness, we choose to ignore some things. We will find that this is quite common in the lives of individuals who thrive off of being stubborn, or having all the answers. Stubbornness and having all the answers to everything will cause limitations to inhibit our ability to grow and learn more. And, the more we become stubborn, the harder life will seem. Stubbornness is not going to get us anywhere; especially, when we have all the answers headed in the wrong direction. Regardless of how much a person may or may not know—there will always be room for improvement. It is very important to become a problem solver, instead of a problem creator. There are some individuals who enjoy being difficult, and being difficult is their way of getting attention. As a matter of fact, their life is a mirror image of their thoughts, emotions, and actions, to say the least. Of course, only God has all the answers, so why not tap into the Source of Divine Wisdom.

Setting boundaries with the right response will keep you in control, regardless of what occurs in your life. This is where balance and integrity come into the picture—having self-control will remove the limits on what you can achieve, as long as you do not get entangled in a web of procrastination.

Procrastinate

The past is not designed to be used as a crutch; it is to be used as a stepping stone. Crutches are basically excuses that leave room for procrastination or taking the easy way out. For the most part, it is very, very hard to achieve anything when we are complacent with doing nothing; besides, it takes up too much energy thinking, worrying or pondering about an excuse anyway.

We all have a natural instinct inside of us that seeks to be understood; especially, by the ones we love. Not to mention, we all have different perceptions, purposes, opinions, and priorities that need to be respected. Of course, understanding can be a lot of things, but it is not rationalizing or judging. As a matter of fact, it is having the patience to see beyond our own point of view. Victories are won by overcoming our fears, limitations or setbacks with our undivided attention. When our attention is divided, it is very hard to take risks or overcome setbacks. When we are satisfied with the way things are, we tend to avoid taking risks—when taking a risk is necessary to get us to the next level.

The best way to start gaining control over our lives is to start controlling what enters our eye gates, ear gates, and what enters or exits the gate of our mouth. As a matter of fact, we often take for granted these 3 gates of entry until our lives spiral out of control. Trust me, an out of control life is not a life of victorious living. In my opinion, a victorious life takes preparation and determination, which are extremely important when it comes down to making the right move at the right time. In addition, our determination begins with us imagining ourselves succeeding or becoming victorious at whatever we do. Of course, determination is all mental; especially when we cannot see, feel, or touch our determination; however, we **CAN** see, feel, and touch the RESULTS of our determination. So, make sure that you keep your mind focused and free of unwanted distractions, to ensure that God places your divine connections where they need to be at the right time.

CHAPTER 17

The Bittersweet Secrets

How do we get through those dry or bitter places in life? A dry/bitter place or drought in life is a time of self-correction. In my opinion, a drought is nature's way of correcting itself to keep Universal Balance and Harmony. This principle is applicable to every aspect of life; therefore, a drought does not enter our lives to kill us—it comes to heal us in places that we are knowingly or unknowingly wounded, handicapped, or disobedient. Of course, we are all a work in progress; however, when we stop progressing in the area of our purpose or when we become codependent, we will find that we will begin to **THIRST** for something or someone that's not conducive to our wellbeing. When we quench our thirst with the wrong thing, it will keep us all over the place mentally and emotionally, it will keep us running to and fro in our busyness accomplishing nothing, or it will keep us wallowing in a bed of indecisiveness that will delay our bountiful harvest. It is best that we take the time to master those dry or thirsty places in our lives to ensure that we do not defy the purpose of our drought.

The Children of Israel travel for three days without water; eventually, they found water at Marah, but the water was bitter. Of course, they complained without fail; however, through our precious commodity of GRACE & MERCY, God told Moses to cast a certain tree into the water, and the water became sweet. Actually, this is God's way of letting us know that He will make provisions for us even when we are being tested as long as we are obedient to His voice.

We will thirst in life, and life will thirst for us until we find a way to quench it. There are indeed many different ways to quench a thirst, and to deal with it our own way is not going to get us to the Promised Land. God is the sustenance of life whether we admit it or not. Even so, in the midst of our lack, He will not tolerate us being ungrateful or resentful for not having the temporary pleasures of life. With that being said, even if our water is bitter right now, it can become sweet if we are willing to take the necessary steps to do so, before we open Pandora's Box.

The act of revenge opens Pandora's Box of bitterness; eventually, causing you to lose value in yourself through compromising your integrity. Revenge is not worth you making bad decisions or losing yourself over. Don't waste your time and energy pondering over how to bring negativity into the life of someone else. Perhaps, you may be justified in being angry; however, it does not justify wrongdoing on your part. The nagging feeling of being a victim will cause bitterness to bite and resentment to sting even worse. Holding on to bitterness and resentment causes mental anguish; basically, it is a silent distraction that keeps you trapped in the past. It also drains your energy, and it puts you in a dangerous position of feeling like a victim. A victimized spirit puts your life in slow motion, and the last thing you want to do is dread living an abundant life. Inner turmoil may come, and it will go if you release the burden of carrying around the exposed bites and bruises of the past.

Instead of seeking revenge, simply allow the situation or circumstance to give you a burst of inspiration to share with others. Everything happens for a reason. Yes, it may hurt. Yes, you may want to get angry. However, saying "NO" to bitterness and resentment is worth preserving your happiness to ensure that you are able to make good, wise decisions. Easier said than done, right? Absolutely, you are going to have to push through those revengeful desires and tendencies. When you feel as if life and people have become your enemy—fight back by letting go and letting God, which will give you the opportunity to seize the moment to be happy.

Bitterness is a byproduct of anger that's caused by disappointment or an unmet expectation. Bitterness comes into play when you allow a negative situation or circumstance to harden your heart toward someone who you felt has wronged you. Refusing to deal with your bitterness causes it to fester and grow until it consumes you, your environment, and your relationships. This is a very serious problem that will destroy you, your marriage, your children, your job, and the list goes on. Bitterness and joy cannot be felt at the same time—it's one or the other, not both. Justifying your bitterness will eventually make matters worse. When you allow bitterness to take root in your heart, it will begin to eat away at your soul, causing you to become a prisoner of your own emotions. Remember, your thoughts, actions, reactions, and feelings will govern whether your life becomes positive, productive, and fruitful. From me to you, don't let your bitterness prevent you from having what belongs to you or take your power from you.

Unforgiveness

The **secret** to everything in life is to trust in God with all your heart and lean not on your own understanding—that is what gives you your POWER. The quickest way to lose your power is through unforgiveness—it is like a ton of bricks weighing you down, draining all of your mental energy. As a matter of fact, unforgiveness is nothing more than holding a grudge; eventually, leaving you angry, bitter, and frustrated with life itself. This could possibly render you incapable of functioning normally due to the constant thoughts of getting even. Of course, no one knows what that person may have done to you, or how that person's actions may have affected you. However, you must think about what unforgiveness is doing to you right now. Don't forgive a person for their sake; forgive them for your sake. Forgiving a person will give you the freedom from inner turmoil, the freedom from bitterness, and most of all, the freedom to be YOU. An unforgiving seed that's planted in your heart will grow into a bitter and resentful tree bearing much fruit. Many of us appearing to have it all together on the outside are afflicted with a known and unknown bitterness that's eating us up from the inside. I personally know how it feels to die a slow death from the inside out in a puddle of unforgiveness and bitterness. This is a very serious problem that will destroy you, your marriage, your children, your job, your church and the list goes on. Beware of your actions, reactions, and body language, because the fruit does not fall far from the tree. If you are harboring bitterness and resentment, it will eventually show up in some area of your life.

Forgiving is the channel through which you can release your deepest hurts and fears. Choosing to forgive does not always mean that you will forget, but it does mean that you will let go of the issue, circumstance, or situation and never bring it up again. As a matter of fact, forgiveness is essential for your growth. Forget about your ego or pride, don't let unforgiveness rob you of your blessings. Every situation in life comes as a teacher, to give you the experience to allow you to grow and flow like never before.

CHAPTER 18

The Fleshly Secrets

As the Children of Israel journeyed through the desert, they became hungry. As usual, they complained to Moses about it—it behooves me that they were willing to go back into bondage and slavery just to fill their stomach with fish, leeks, onions, garlic, melons, and cucumbers at no cost. They did not realize that it wasn't really for free! However, Moses prayed to God, despite their vicious complaints, and God rained bread from heaven, which is commonly known as "Manna." God also gave them many different ways to prepare the manna, and the Children of Israel were still not satisfied—they wanted more. They wanted meat, if God intended for them to live off of meat, He would have rained down meat instead of manna or meat in conjunction with the manna. In fact, having meat was never God's original plan for them. God's first plan was THE PROMISED LAND with MILK AND HONEY! His second plan was to feed them bread from heaven. He was trying to deal with their slave mentality, and they were focused on their next meal, oppose to their next step. They spoke of freedom and continually thought about slavery—this is definitely an indication that the price of bricks and mud was more valuable to them than the freedom to create a life of whatever they wanted.

After the Children of Israel constantly complained to Moses about meat, God gave them meat to feed their fleshly cravings. He did not give them meat for one day as He does with the daily ration of manna—He gave them meat for a whole month. While giving into the murmurs and the lust of their flesh, they overindulged by partaking too much of something that they were not supposed to have anyway. By this one act of greed, eating the meat caused a plague that took the lives of many. As a result, they still did not get the big picture; which provides us with an opportunity to go right, where they went wrong.

The wilderness experience is designed to purge you from the desires of wanting or giving in to your fleshly desires. GOD HEARS ALL MURMURS and now is not the time to murmur about what you don't have; this is a time of soul-searching to understand the deeper meaning of the Manna that's presented in your life. What was "Manna" in the Old Testament is now your "Spiritual Guide" in the New Testament". Going through this phase, you will definitely have to walk by faith, and not by sight as you allow this to become your Bread of Life. Jesus tells us about the value of our daily bread in the Sermon on the Mount saying, "Give us this day our daily bread," in Matthew 6:11 of the Lord's Prayer; however, it still goes overlooked, day in and day out! Our daily portion is a PRAYER, and if we gather up enough, is it not the Bread of Life? A big prayer or little prayer, it is a Prayer—the only difference is how we view it! Our Blessings are indeed hidden in plain sight—when we live our lives out of purpose, or when we live our lives in some sort of bondage, it creates a life that's full of limitations and excuses that hinder our ability to embrace our purpose or passion.

UNDERSTANDING YOUR MANNA

For forty years the Children of Israel ate the heavenly food called Manna. They were instructed to take only what they needed for their daily ration, and when they failed to follow God's specific instructions, their daily ration would rot, and worms would appear. They barely recognized that this was a provision of the Lord; and regardless of their disobedience, it never stopped coming. I considered the Manna as being the sanctifying tool that God used to process Egypt out of the Children of Israel. Okay, let me explain, the Children of Israel were **saved** out of and from Egypt; so there was no reason for God to save them from the desert because they were already saved. God's intent was to sanctify them in the desert through the use of Manna and then, take them into the Promised Land flowing with milk and honey. Of course, that did not happen until 40 years later, but we do not have to wait 40 years to maximize the information that they left behind!

Manna basically means, "What is it?" When we truly understand how the answer to this simple question impacts our lives, it will definitely teach us how to live on supernatural substance opposed to superficial facades. Believe it or not, it is through your Manna which is now called your **Wilderness Experience** that God will test you to see how you would handle hardship, stress, lack, and success. For example, if you ever find yourself with an inner hunger for something and you don't know what it is, you must ask yourself, what is it? What's the problem? What areas in my life that I need to be strengthened in? What areas do I need to become obedient? What areas do I need to exercise patience? What areas of my life do I need to persevere? Regardless of what question you ask, it must be concluded with "In Jesus' Name." As Jesus states very clearly, *"I am the bread of life. He who comes to Me shall never hunger, and he who believes in Me shall never thirst." John 6:35.*

The Children of Israel were also instructed to collect the Manna in the morning, which I find very symbolic. If you gather your Manna (get your daily instructions through prayer) in the morning, God will give you what you need for that day to get you through the testing and trials. So, there is no reason to find fault in people, places, and things that are designed to propel you—simply take what you need, without finding fault in it, and move on.

In the wandering process, hope was lost with the Children of Israel; therefore, giving you an opportunity to ensure that your hope lives on. Now, in order to hone in on our hope, we must never take our eyes off the promise. We must focus, focus, and focus some more to ensure that our hand, mind, and eye coordination is in its proper sequence. What that means is that your eyes must be focused in the same direction as your mind; while your hands work toward the common goal that your mind and your eyes envision. Just remember, life has a way of catering to you as long as you KNOW what you want, want what you have, maximize your daily portion of manna, and here is the **BIG SECRET**: we must FAST. Why is it such a secret? I will tell you, as it is written in Matthew 17:21, "Some things can only come out by fasting and prayer."

FASTING

The HIDDEN SECRET about healing our bodies mentally, physically, emotionally, and spiritually is through fasting. It has what I call a Four-Fold Effect—Mind, Body, Soul, and Spirit. We do not need to just fast for the body—we must fast for the other areas as well to ensure that there's balance and harmony between all of them. Although, we are taught to fear fasting; however, our bodies are designed to do it. And, due to the fact that we are not fasting as we should, our nation has become riddled with diseases and sicknesses that are at epidemic levels now.

Biblically, we are supposed to fast and pray, but we do not—we will pray; however, we will not give up food. Most of us think that fasting is just about fasting food out of our lives, but fasting is much more than just that. Fasting is purging anything out of our lives that we don't want, or bring life to what we do want in our lives through prayer and sacrifice. If we want love, make a sacrifice of giving it. If we have an anger problem, make a sacrifice of not becoming angry. If we have a problem arguing, make a sacrifice of not arguing. If the urge comes, you must go to your **SECRET PLACE** to pray. The power of fasting has been around since the beginning of time, and it's not going anywhere because it's the best form of healing known to man, as well as animals. It allows the body to rest, while it detoxifies and heal itself. When we allow our bodies to fast, it will heal the common diseases, getting rid of bacteria, waste products, toxins, tumors, fibroids, viruses, mucus, plaque, inflammation, and stored fat. This is the safest way for the body to heal itself, plus it is indeed the way our bodies were created from the beginning of time.

We must condition our bodies to fast at least 2-times a week if possible. This will give our bodies a break, and it will give our bodies time to detoxify itself because viruses love to cling to the colon; and if we are not careful, we will set ourselves up for defeat because the viruses can pass into our blood stream as foreign protein. Remember, toxins, bacteria, and viruses are everywhere, and we cannot get away from it—it's in the meat, on our vegetables, in our food, etc. Fasting helps get rid of the mucus buildup in your body as well. It is through the mucus that viruses, bacteria, and parasites hide, feed, and thrive, spreading illnesses throughout our bodies to breakdown our immune system to take over the same way that they did to the Children of Israel.

This story has a fountain of Hidden Wisdom that goes unaccounted for—but, if we would dare to take a moment to understand what we are putting in our bodies affect us mentally, emotionally, physically, and most of all, spiritually. Make no mistake about it, fasting and prayer can rout any sort of stronghold, demon, or bondage faster than anything known to man; or better yet, anything under the sun. Instead of us running to alcohol, cigarettes, pills, food, or sex for comfort—why not run to fasting for solutions? Trust me, when we fast and pray for the right reasons without murmuring, counting it all joy—Wisdom will bow down, Spiritual Enlightenment will bow down, Spiritual Favor will bow down, the Spiritual Veil will bow down to cover us, and the Holy Spirit will bow down to guide us in the right direction, GUARANTEED. Bowing down is not used here in a negative way, it is used as a form of a yielding process to ensure that the seen and unseen people, places, and things that are not good for us, will PASSOVER us. And, if we have a desire for the unseen Spiritual Forces of the Nature of God to bow down to us, we must bow down in fasting and prayer. This is done by becoming humble first, and then putting our fleshly desires under subjection in PRIVATE. What that means is that we must not publicly display our fasting—this is between the fastee and our Heavenly Father.

There are many different types of fast; however, one must go to God in prayer to determine the type of fast that's appropriate for the situation, circumstance, event, or the lack thereof. However, once the decision is made....don't look back.

CHAPTER 19

The Secrets of NOT Looking Back

The Children of Israel walked toward the Promised Land with Egypt on their mind. Have you ever tried to walk forward with your head turned back? They repeatedly tripped over themselves mentally, because they were focusing their attention in the wrong direction. I personally believe that they should have been focusing their attention on God, who brought them out of Egypt. However, I also understand that mental enslavement has a way of causing the best of us to reminisce about the things of old. Now, my question is, are you looking back into the past for temporary comfort? Are you set in your own ways? Do you feel as if you are always right, and everyone else is wrong? If you answered, "yes" to any one of these questions, you are headed toward a lifestyle that is resistant to change; therefore, causing you to become stuck in your own Egypt mentally.

When breaking the slave mentality you have two

choices: 1. Become a slave to quick fixes. 2. Become a master over the situations, circumstances, and conditions in your life. Now, in order to be more, see more, do more, and have more, we must find a way to take our mind out of Egypt. As a matter of fact, unreleased emotional frustrations from our past mistakes can and will cause us to fear what the future holds.

When we encounter a road block in our lives, it does not necessarily mean that it's the wrong way, it is possible that all we need to do is move some things around, or out of the way. However, there are times when we turn around instead of finding out what's blocking us, or whether we are able to remove the blocks to ensure that we are able to continue on. In fact, sometimes turning around and giving up is our subconscious mind's way of secretly beating the notion of preconceived failure.

I know that no one really wants to fail, but if we do, **So What**! Just learn from it and move on; however, thinking that we are going to fail before we do, is not wise thinking. One of the worse experiences that we could ever encounter is to give up on ourselves too soon. The appearance of failure could very well be our success in disguise. From me to you, finish what you start! Whether you succeed or not, make sure it's done, and the lesson is learned to ensure that history does not repeat itself or develop a blind spot in your life.

Blind Spot

Blind Spots have a way of inhibiting our vision, causing us to trip over things that we should already have under our feet. Let me ask you, "Have you ever tripped over something that you knew was on the floor, but for some odd reason you overlooked it and tripped anyway?" I know; we all have! However, an unexpected stumble gives us a quick reason to make the appropriate adjustments to ensure that we keep ourselves from falling. Actually, there are certain things in life that we will be able to see, and there are certain things that we don't want to see. Tripping over a blind spot in our lives does not necessarily mean that there is nothing there. As odd as it may seem, that may be God's way of testing us, our vision, our ability to accept rejection, our ability to let go, our willingness to forgive, our willingness to take a risk, our willingness to be laughed at, and our ability to celebrate others. Furthermore, becoming goal oriented is risky business; therefore, we must get some things under our feet and keep them there. If not, fear and distractions are waiting at the door to block or blind the creative force that's inside of us.

Assuming responsibility with the willingness to take action will help prevent you from tripping over people, places, and things that are in your blind spot. Oh, by the way, when you find the hidden value in your stumble, it makes the stumble well worth it—just remember to keep those unwanted distractions under your feet as you focus on loving the skin you are in.

CHAPTER 20

The Secret Enemy From Within

The greatest battle for the Children of Israel was the battle with the enemy from within. They were so caught up in dwelling on the negative that they became totally blind to the positive. Pharaoh had created so much emotional damage that they fought themselves, struggling to find their own identity. Furthermore, it seems as if the Children of Israel were fighting against Moses, but that really was not the case. They were really fighting against themselves and took it out on Moses, as he seemed to be the ideal target. By doing so, they placed limits all around them—they limited themselves, they limited Moses and most of all, they limited God.

Most often, when there is inner turmoil, we strike out at other people oppose to striking out against ourselves. Now, my question to you is, "Who is your enemy?" Is it Satan? No, it is not! Satan may use people, places, and things to get to you, but he is not your enemy in this game. The key to winning is assuming responsibility for your own role in your life. This may seem hard to swallow; however, the truth must be revealed, the real enemy is inside of you—the (inner me) enemy. For that reason, this is not the time to become closed-minded!

The area in your life that irritates you the most will be the area that you need to work on the most. Since your life is in 3-D, it will always be up close and personal. How do you get rid of an issue that's always in your face? It's going to take THE 3-D EFFECT: discipline, direction, and determination. Seeing the invisible possibilities of your life may not be an easy task, but it becomes easier when you open your mind's eye. What is the mind's eye? The mind's eye is basically your imagination. A well-controlled imagination can work wonders in your life. Seeing the impossible is just a choice away. There will be a lot of things that you may not be able to do, but there are a lot of things that you can do as long as you can see it and believe it mentally. Actually, it is through the mind that we are able to make a choice to free ourselves from the fear of failure, limitations, insecurities, concerns, and worries. However, it is imperative that you look at everything differently. No more cat and mouse games with yourself. The excitement of chasing things is not so exciting when you get what you want, and it is not what you expected. Be careful about your wants and needs, because the satisfaction may not last too long after you get it; and, it may create a desire for more of what you don't want or need.

There are times when we hate to do a self-analysis, but it is mandatory. As a matter of fact, self-correction will usually prevent an individual from making the **same** mistakes over and over again. Please do not misunderstand me, mistakes are inevitable at times; however, trials and obstacles are sometimes designed to propel you into greatness. One of the most obvious signs of progress is when you are able to take an embarrassing or a not so good moment in your life, learn from it, and turn it into something positive. Today is your golden opportunity to follow-up, learn, and position yourself for the best. Besides, you deserve it; you never want negative shadows to follow you for the rest of your life.

The Vice

The price of entertaining your vice can break you in more ways than one. Your vices are NOT meant to be entertained. A vice is basically a bad habit that usually causes a serious urge of discontentment or a desire for more. As a matter of fact, it will also cause you to seek immediate gratification to fill that silent void from within. It is the unresolved vices that break up homes, families, friendships and causes confusion on the job. Believe it or not, it takes the same amount of energy to form a good or bad habit; basically, it's really all about CHOICES. Where you are today is a result of your past decisions—now, the time has come for you to let go of the past, and embrace the creativity that you have harbored for years. Actually, taking action today will enable you to take a step away from your vice and into a balanced lifestyle conquering those Mind Germs that have tried to contaminate your thought process.

We have a natural instinct that's embedded inside of us to want and desire more out of life. However, little annoyances and vexing distractions are hidden triggers that are designed to throw us off balance. When we are annoyed or distracted, most often we are too busy judging the situation or circumstance instead of trying to understand it. Nevertheless, you do have a few choices when annoyances and distractions are presented in your life:

1. Focus on something positive.
2. Allow it to have a negative impact on your life.

Obstacles are not designed for us to stare at them; they are designed so that we can look beyond them. And, trust me, now is not the time for fidgeting over yesterday's mistakes, we must find a way to reclaim control over the things that are secretly driving us insane. In order to do so, it is best to try a little love, patience, and kindness. This will always give us the upper hand when it comes down to those hidden triggers.

When you feel yourself becoming annoyed or distracted, just take a second to count your blessings to ensure that you do not sabotage what God has graciously bestowed upon you. Character flaws are usually revealed under pressure when our stress level is intensified. Everyone will have some form of stress or flaws in his or her life; some will use their stress or flaws as a driving force, and some will use them as a reason to give up. Nevertheless, overreacting while under stress could lead to the defamation of your own character. What you do over a period of time, how you react over a period of time, or how you treat yourself over a period of time, will be the determining factor(s) revealing wholeness or emptiness in your character. Character is of great importance in your life; some people may not care about their character—yet, you should. I am not saying that you should be driven by the opinions of others; however, I am saying that you should be driven by your own opinion of yourself. With that being said, do what you have to do and never let them see you sweat.

Doubt

Being side-tracked by doubt creates an open door for your inner critic to control your life. When doubt is in control, it has enough power to stop a person right in his or her tracks without them even realizing it. For this reason, it is very important to stay ahead of the game when it comes down to doubt, because it does not travel alone—it comes with the immediate family, ancestors, and friends of emotional bondage. Doubt is a simple thought, creating limitations and insecurities within oneself. Now my question is when doubt comes knocking at your door, who is your worst critic? Could it possibly be you? Maybe or maybe not, but if you leave room for doubt in your life, your inner critic can and will cause you to become envious, insecure, and miserable. However, when you take positive action, it erases doubt; therefore, bringing forth the confidence that will create an atmosphere for you to succeed without being sidetracked. SUCCESS is not based on how much you know—it is based on your determination to learn more than you did the day before and how well you are able to deal with the Enemy Inside of Y.O.U.

Anger

Mismanaged anger will cause you to lose out on your promise, as did Moses in his battle with his anger. Now, if the truth is told, anger is considered to be a hidden vice of not getting your own way. Society in itself has a knack of overlooking this destructive emotion. When in all actuality, this hidden vice is the epitome of divided relationships today. For example, losing your temper through rage or explosive anger is a telltale sign of being out of control. Just look around you, anger has killed more relationships than any other emotion on the face of this earth. And, it is for that very reason, it is imperative that you think about the consequences first, before making a choice to become angry.

It is so amazing to me, how anger will cause us to lose out on what we really want; when patience is the KEY to having our way. An outburst of anger diminishes your strength and not to mention your self-control. This also gives the person, place, or thing control over your emotions—keeping you in a state of disarray or on an emotional roller-coaster with your permission to do so. And, once again, it only takes a few seconds to pray before you react. There is no need to have a long drawn out prayer when you need immediate assistance—just say, "Help me, Lord" or "Holy Spirit, take over." Even when you keep it simple, it is just as EFFECTIVE, and it will work wonders in your life!

What do you gain from becoming or staying angry all the time? You will gain frustration, depression, anxiety, feeling sorry for yourself, resentfulness, helplessness, and the list goes on with negative attributes. Once consumed by these emotions, self-destruction is around the corner waiting for you to give in. The frustrations of life are designed to keep you off balance; and, rest assured that you know better than anyone else what triggers you to become angry or irate. However, in order to overcome anger, it has to be replaced with something positive, such as compassion.

Compassion is what's needed to empower and strengthen you to forgive and let go of the desire to stay angry. This may be your test or the deciding factor of whether or not you are entitled to your blessing. Just remember, a positive attitude will enable you to discover incredible opportunities that will enhance your life for the better. From me to you, keep your mind free and clear of all unwanted emotions, while understanding that no one can make you angry unless you choose to be angry. You are responsible for your own actions and reactions. Don't give in and let anger get the best of you and deprive you of your blessing(s) or cause you to argue.

HANDLING YOUR ANGER:

1. Refuse to yell, scream, fuss or fight when you are angry.
2. Recognize and admit that you are angry.
3. Recognize what or who caused the anger.
4. Refuse to lay blame and accept responsibility for your anger.
5. Pray about the feeling and why you are feeling that way.

6. Forgive and let go of it.

Distractions

Giving in to things that break your daily interactions with yourself and your goals will deplete your strength over a period of time if you allow it. Is there something in your life that keeps breaking your concentration, over and over again? Yes, No, or you don't know? Well, it is time to find out, because if you don't fix it early, it will fix you later! How do you fix it? Become aware of the breached or unguarded area(s) of your life. Then, pray and make the necessary arrangements with God to repair the damage before it sweeps you away. Your breach or unguarded area could be a job, a relationship, your family, a habit, a weakness, your choice of lifestyle, etc. Trust me when I tell you this, it is hard to regain your balance when you are blindsided by something you took for granted. True recognition comes when you appreciate who you are from within, making every moment count.

Recognition is something that we usually expect from others; however, it should be something that we give to ourselves, first. Being able to recognize the true essence of who you are, has much more power than you can ever imagine. From me to you, steer clear of wasteful conflict that's out of character for you. This will help you appreciate yourself without diminishing your effectiveness. Start valuing your time to ensure that it's not wasted on unproductive things. Always remember, your blessing(s) will not depend on someone's ability to recognize you, accept you, or make you happy—it is determined based on your own ability to be happy, as well as your ability to recognize and accept yourself for who you are!

CHAPTER 21

The Secret Of Holy Hands

As the Children of Israel journeyed through the desert, they had to deal with a war without provocation from the Amalekites at Rephidim, according to Exodus 17:8-13. They went into battle as Moses prays with his rod lifted up. Basically, their success was based on Moses' ability to keep that rod uplifted toward Heaven. For that reason, the Children of Israel defeated the Amalekites. The key to this battle is the lifting of Holy Hands in prayer like Moses did when they fought. *For this battle, you will not win with your ability to fight; you will win with your ability to pray! Galatians 5:17.* Yet, after all of this, they still complained.

Unfortunately, as they journeyed through the desert, many were being bitten by poisonous snakes and dying. Once again, they begged Moses for help, and like old faithful, he prayed. God told him to make a copper snake and place it on a pole. If anyone gets bitten, they would need only to look at this copper snake, and they would not die. Now, as we bring this into today's reality, when we are dealing with any situation, look at the cross. Jesus died for our sins, giving us the opportunity to work out our vices to get rid of the bandits in our life.

You may ask yourself, "Would God really provide enough for me to survive during this wilderness experience." The answer is "YES!" Remember, there is no lack—God will provide! Now, are you willing to trust Him? Your SUCCESS will not be based on how much you know—it will be based upon your determination to use what you already have to defeat the bandits. From my own personal experiences, I have found that it is Satan's job to keep us defeated. And, it is also his job to send out these little bandits to ensure that we sabotage our own success, through our own self-destructive ways and habits

How can you tell if you are spiritually in sync or on the right track? Life is full of trial and error, ups and downs, happiness and disappointments, fun times and not so great times, etc; however, when we are on a Spiritual Journey, if we are on the right path, or whatever we are trying to obtain that's in alignment with our purpose, life has a way of making provisions for us. In my opinion, the best way that I have found that I am on the right track is when I think of something without verbalizing it in the natural, and it's provided automatically. For those who do not understand what I'm talking about, let me break it down a little bit further; for example, if I have a need for a certain item to fulfill a certain purpose, I would not verbalize my need to any person, nor will I verbalize the need in prayer; what I would actually do is verbalized my need from within and then I let the thought go or better yet, I set my need free to allow the Universe to provide that particular need. If God feels as if I do not need it, He will not provide it; but, if He feels as if I need it and it is good for me, He will provide it by sending me right to it, He will enable someone to bring it to me, or provide Supernatural favor regarding whatever that "IT" is. This is called Spiritual Intuition or Spiritually Synced, if we are not on that path or Journey, then this wouldn't mean anything; however, if one is on that Journey, this tad bit of information is going to bring confirmation.

When we become spiritually connected, our wants, needs, and desires that are conducive to our purpose are provided for us; which doesn't mean that we can become lackadaisical about what we need to do, it doesn't mean that we can become arrogant, and it doesn't mean that we have to become co-dependent. What it means is that we must be willing to do what it takes to get to where we need to be, and allow God to do the rest without us stressing ourselves out regarding people, places, and things that we cannot change. All of our needs, wants, and desires are provided for us, and if they are not, it is imperative that we check the REASON behind our wants, desires, and needs. Coveting, jealousy, and envy are not the criteria that allow the flow of Spiritual Abundance. Therefore, it is imperative that we do not become greedy, selfish, and hateful—those are a few characteristics that will cause our blessings to elude us.

Today, let nothing or no one separate you from the presence of your Heavenly Father. He is indeed a provider, He is indeed your help in your time of need, He is indeed the one that loves you unconditionally, and He will be the one that will take care of you no matter what. Although people change; but hear me when I say this, He will NOT; He's the same yesterday, today, and forever more. "I am young, and now I am old, I have not seen the righteous forsaken, nor their children begging for bread." Psalms 37:25. From me to you, Trust and Believe that all things will work together for your good.

CHAPTER 22

The Measurement Secrets

Moses went into the wilderness to pray for 40 days; he did not tell anyone how long he would be gone. He basically wanted them to believe in God, or to simply have faith in His deliverance. Of course, the Children of Israel became impatient like usual. They coerced Aaron into erecting a golden calf—to me; that confirmed that their hearts were still in Egypt. They had indeed picked up the Egyptian culture, even though they were in denial. The Children of Israel wanted Moses to be perfect, not realizing that if he was perfect, then he would not have a need to pray. Or, better yet, He would not have a need to allow God to guide him in the way that they should go. Even through the erection of the golden calf, they did not realize that it wasn't perfect as well, nor could it intercede on their behalf.

When God's voice is silent, who will we listen to? This is a perfect example of how we can become knowingly or unknowingly influenced by our environment and the people, places and things around us. Rest assured that God will deal with the idols in our life—we will definitely have to take an account for our behavior, or what we privately worship when no one's looking. Being polite or tiptoeing around this issue as Aaron did, is not wise and it will eventually cause some sort of embarrassment as God will deal with:

1. Our flesh.
2. Our wishy-washy nature.
3. Our willingness to compromise.
4. Our belief system.
5. Our impatience.

The Golden Calf was a symbolic way of telling God that they did not trust Him. This showed a picture-perfect act of rebellion that was fueled by pride, anger, doubt, selfishness, fear, and weakness.

The Difference
God has strategically written a tablet of the 10 commandments on every person's heart, whether we know it or not. Even though we are saved by grace, the 10 commandments are designed to help bring structure, order, and guidance into the lives of those who believe. The commandments are not designed to put us in a box or boss us around; it's designed to encourage us without posing any type of threat. It also prepares us for our blessings, and how not to bring about an unwanted curse into our lives; therefore, giving us an opportunity to set limits and boundaries. More importantly, it will help you to make

sense of your **small blessings** as well, because when you measure light against light, you can hardly see a difference; but, if you measure light against darkness, it's like night and day. This is exactly what the 10 commandments will do for you. Simply measure your life against it and see what you come up with.

Doing the Dirty Work

Getting your hands dirty is not so bad when you are planting seeds in fertile ground. There are times when you are going to have to do the dirty work. I am not speaking of dirty work in a negative way; I am just referring to the dirty work as doing something that you or others may not want to do. There will be a lot of things that will be beneath you and your abilities, but this does not give you an excuse for not doing what it takes to make it happen.

We often dread being disciplined in certain areas of our lives; but, in my opinion, it's the most undisciplined areas that are constantly throwing us off track. What we will find is that the lack of discipline will paralyze us in the area(s) that we are supposed to excel in. This is something that will eventually get out of control and stunt our growth if it is not put under control quickly. Whatever this undisciplined area of our life is, it must be exposed and dealt with accordingly, because most of our bountiful blessing(s) come in a package that we would assume not to open.

Assumptions come, and assumptions go; however, just because you assume something, does not necessarily make it fact! Assuming that something's wrong will sometimes cause the joke to be on you, so be extremely careful. A negative assumption is the one detouring factor that causes most of us to miss out on great opportunities. Negative assumptions are designed to create mental blocks that cause us to rationalize, justify, and judge the people, places, and things that appear to be contradicting the things that we desire. Please understand that things change all around us and within us as the seasons do. God will not rush you into making any unwise decisions through assumptions; it is Satan that tries to push you into getting ahead of God. However, there is no need for panic; simply, replace your assumptions with spiritual alertness, allowing your spirit man to look for the hidden value of something that most people would actually overlook or throw to the side.

CHAPTER 23

The Secrets of Ill-Gotten Gain

As the Children of Israel went into Jericho, God gave specific instructions not to take anything; but, Achan took some stuff for himself and buried it in his tent. This was a great act of disobedience for him and the Children of Israel, which caused them to lose the battle at Ai. It's amazing how one bad seed will spoil the whole bunch. As a result, the Children of Israel had to eliminate Achan, his family and all of his belongings. What a waste! The same people who lift you up today could possibly, knowingly or unknowingly, let you down tomorrow. For that reason, when moving to possess your promise, you must find a way to leave the tainted stuff behind. In this phase, God will provide all of your needs—you will have your own stuff! God is going to bless what you have, and not what you **take**; but your **consistent obedience** to Him will be required to obtain **consistent results** from Him!

The ill-gotten gain will cause many individuals to become

a slave to continual compromise. Compromise is not always composed of taking shortcuts or the easy way out of things. Sometimes, a compromise will reside in the things that you enjoy the most, making it very important to consider the people, places, and things in your life. Gain out of dishonesty will eventually find itself some wings and fly away. Don't misunderstand me; there's a little give and take in everything that you do; but, if you are on the take more than you give, then you will eventually have problems. It is more profitable to pay the price on the front-end to ensure you have your blessings on the back-end. Your best bet is, to be honest with yourself and others to prevent any unwanted compromises that will cause you to suffer or endure a loss later on down the line. There is no reason to become needy—just allow the abundance of God to fill your life.

A little give and take are needed to ensure that you do not overdo or drain yourself when your reputation is on the line. It is amazing how your reputation can be shattered so quickly by not following through. Never set yourself up for self-obliteration, your reputation is more precious than fine gold. As a matter of fact, what appears to be a great reputation without God can be shattered in a fraction of a second? In my opinion, your reputation is worth more than temporary gratification. Just remember, blessings will come your way when you least expect it if you are able to embrace the opportunity to turn a negative situation into something positive.

CHAPTER 24

The Secret Behind Difficult People

The easiest way to deal with difficult people is to open up the opportunity to deal with self, first. There will be those who are really hard to get along with, and there will be those who think that you are hard to get along with as well. Regardless of whether you are difficult or not, it will always be a matter of opinion. Difficult people are not really difficult; they are just a little different. The people that are a little different does not always require a response from you; they just need you to understand and respect their differences. A person that's constantly judged as being difficult will appear to become more difficult over a period of time. However, it's just an illusion—they are the best teachers in disguise. Hint, hint, they are the ones who most often possess hidden values that are only revealed when they are not judged, ridiculed, or forced to change. Take a look at self first, and then change how you view those who appear to be difficult and watch how the doors of opportunity start to swing open.

The credence of our words has enough power to crush even the strongest person when caught off guard. This is what happened when Miriam, the sister of Moses, caught him off guard with her outburst of anger. Soon thereafter, Miriam became plagued with leprosy and had to be put out of the camp for 7 days. This seems like very harsh treatment for someone who criticized her brother, right? Wrong, Miriam was a prophetess—she knew better; she knew firsthand how God spared Moses, she also knew about what happened to Pharaoh and the plagues that brought them out of Egypt. We as a people, need to be very cautious when speaking against a person who is doing the Will of God.

This story is so applicable to our lives today—we bring about plagues in our lives because we cannot control our tongue. Most often, it is our attitude that causes us to get put out of the camp. Our best bet is to take the lead with all confidence as we set a guard over what comes out of our mouth.

Taking the Lead

On the final stage of their journey, God told Moses to choose a lead representative from each of the 12 tribes to spy out the land of Canaan; which meant from God's point of view—they all had something different to offer. After spying out the land for 40 days, they brought back huge grapes along with pomegranates and figs to confirm that their Promised Land was indeed flowing with milk and honey. However, there was one big problem—10 of the 12 spies brought back a negative report. All, except

Joshua and Caleb, spoke about Giants in the Land of Canaan—they did not believe that they could possess the land, so they placed fear in God's chosen people.

After all God had done for them, they forgot the promise that He made when He said, *"And I will send an angel before thee; and I will drive out the Canaanite, the Amorite, and the Hittite, and the Perizzite, the Hivite, and the Jebusite."* *Exodus 33:2.* Wobbly faith will not stand against an enemy who gains his or her power from fearful people. The goal was not to take the land; their goal was to possess the land, which meant taking up residence in a place that belonged to them anyway.

This is God's way of getting us to see the vision before it takes place in our lives. He will allow us to chart out our territory; regardless of whether someone else occupies it or not. Anything that's worth having will have a giant protecting it; and, this is where we have to become very strategic. God has a way of sending us out to get the information first before He blesses us. In so many words, He really wants to see what we are going to do with the information we obtain and whether or not we are going to add faith to it.

CHAPTER 25

The Secret Murmur

The act of murmuring is basically the refusal of our promise. Most often, we find ourselves complaining about people, places, and things that we do not believe in. As a result of the Children of Israel refusing their promise, they wondered in the wilderness for 40 years, 1 year for every day that the spies were in Canaan.

How often do we speak before we think about what we are saying? Quite often, right? Absolutely. The individuals that are out of control verbally are setting themselves up for a great disappointment, SOCIALLY! Of course, some people may not say anything when they are offended; but eventually, their actions will speak louder than the words that were spoken to them. Every word that comes out of your mouth has power—the power to infuse and the power to deflate. The difference between the two is CHOICE. You choose your own words! Becoming selective in your words will cause you to become more selective in your thoughts, actions, and reactions. As a matter of fact, well-chosen words will also boost your ability to communicate effectively with yourself. Simply, take a second to actually listen to yourself speak, because it's impossible to be in control of your life when the gate of your mouth is out of control.

The quickest way to find alienation is to put down someone, opposed to building them up. Constructive criticism is not a bad thing—it builds the lives of others; however, destructive criticism is a different story—it destroys the lives of others. Destroying the lives of others is a sure way of reaping havoc in your life. The people who call you crazy, criticize, or belittle you will most often find himself or herself with a constant flow of people in and out of their lives. If people laugh at you for following your heart, ignore them. If people call you crazy for following your heart, ignore them. If people belittle you for following your heart, ignore them and take time out to build the lives of others. As a matter of fact, this is a sure way of activating the law of reciprocity to improve as well as enhance your own life.

Your attitude will determine whether you stay on top of things or sink to the bottom. If you want to determine someone's quality of life, just pay attention to his or her attitude. A negative attitude reveals doom & gloom in any circumstance opposed to a positive attitude that reveals hope in the midst of unfortunate circumstances. I must add, a positive attitude may not bring you health, wealth, and success; however, it will give you the strength and wisdom needed to keep you from sinking to the bottom of the barrel.

The words that come out of your mouth will determine the amount of wisdom that you possess from within. Wisdom is not confrontational, and it does not make you come across as if you have a chip on your shoulder. With wisdom, there is no need to argue, just make your point and leave it alone. Yes, it is easier said than done—you may feel justified to argue; however, arguing will not solve the problem.

Thinking rationally before you speak will always put you in full control over yourself as well as the situation at hand. An out of control tongue will lead to an out of control life; it's just a matter of time. Always remember that it takes two to argue and only one to fuss; whichever end you are on—they are both negative. I have found throughout the years that the reason we have negative attitudes is basically due to anger, unforgiveness, jealousy, envy, greed, fear, and resentment. Stay positive and create a positive environment for everyone you come in contact with. A positive attitude will enable you to discover incredible opportunities that will enhance your life for the better.

POWER-STRUGGLE

Power struggles are another reason to be placed outside the camp. When everyone wants to be in control at the same time, it causes chaos and confusion that disrupts the harmony among all involved. In Moses' case, he was refused the opportunity to go into the Promised Land because of his struggle with his anger. The power struggle that he had from within caused him to angrily strike the rock twice, after the Children of Israel kept complaining about being thirsty. As a result, He was overcome with anger, he had just buried his sister Miriam and yet, they still complained about their unhappiness.

When we find ourselves overworking to stay in control, we will soon suffer from some form of burnout. Burnout creates undue stress affecting everyone in our lives; as a matter of fact, increased stress levels in our body also creates other issues such as insomnia, depression, extreme fatigue, and lack of focus; which have negative effects. One rule of thumb, when you work—you work and when it's time to go to bed—go to bed! Is it possible to turn work off? Absolutely! It is all about choice; you have ultimate control over your thoughts. Burnout has a way of causing you to do or say things that will bring your show to a complete halt.

Intentionally looking for faults in other people, places, and things is a quick way to destroy our own blessings. Furthermore, before we pass judgment regarding anyone or anything—it is imperative that we take a quick reflection over our own lives, to make sure that we are not judging someone to cover up something that we are denying or have denied for years. If someone is doing a great job, tell him or her. If someone is making a change for the better, tell him or her. Whatever it is, compliment them. Compliment, Compliment, Compliment! And from me to you, the quickest way into the heart of anyone, is to encourage him or her positively, regardless of his or her faults or vices—just make sure that it is sound, just, and biblically accurate. If you are involved in a power-struggle right now, or on the verge of a burnout—delegate, prioritize, relax, or release your attachments to it to prevent yourself from an undue lash-out.

Show Stoppers

Lashing out at others is one of the quickest ways to sabotage your credibility with someone, or bring your show to a complete stop. As a matter of fact, speaking out of anger has been the catalyst of our downfall. When we are hurting, we tend to hurt others without realizing it. This is not always a bad thing, if we are aware of it, to make the corrections necessary to change the atmosphere to a positive one. The best way to effectively get your point across is to react calmly; besides, it only takes a fraction of a second to adjust your response mechanism. Anger should never push you to the point where you attack someone with physical or verbal abuse—you do not have to scream, fuss, fight, or slam doors and hope that the other person will get the hint. Tell him or her, so that he or she may know what is causing your spirit to be disrupted. Expressing anger is a natural, healthy response and is necessary to keep your emotions balanced out. Keep your mind free and clear of all unwanted emotions, while understanding that no one can make you angry unless you choose to be angry. You are responsible for your own actions and reactions; so, don't give in and let anger get the best of you.

It is important to learn when to speak and when to listen. The right words at the right time will encourage someone; but on the other hand, the wrong words at the wrong time can discourage, or damage someone for a lifetime. If you have not noticed, the way you start a conversation will usually determine how it will end. As you continue to live in a world where communication is vital, you must know that you are held accountable for every word that comes out of your mouth—known and unknown. Thinking before you speak is a vital resource needed to be able to get your point across without using words that hurt people. Yes, some people are more sensitive than others, and some people are just indifferent. Regardless of how a person is perceived—an encouraging word WILL pierce the heart of the most sensitive person, all the way to the rock solid person. So speak the truth in love, choosing your words carefully with a positive outlook, and you will always find the right words to say at the right time.

We can only hold ourselves together for so long without self-correction. When or if we develop a non-correctional attitude, we will soon start getting our confidence confused with arrogance or pride. The Bible speaks about this very firmly; this is a state that God strictly warns us against called "The Pride of Life." Moreover, this is the quickest way to fall flat on our face with no one to pick us up. Arrogance and pride are sure signs of weakness! In so many words, an arrogant or prideful individual cannot really learn anything, simply because they think that they know it all. Quite often, we will find that a know-it-all individual obviously wastes time and energy boosting their ego. Yes, there are times when we want our way, but we must understand that it may or may not be the right way. Whether we feel right or wrong about our way of doing things, we must not leave the presence of God looking for or trying to create our own blessings. In every circumstance in our lives come an opportunity to create something positive and productive. No matter what you are going through—if you never give up on God, He will never give up on you. From me to you, humility is one **secret** that you do not want to miss on your Journey! This will help prevent a life of pure drama.

Forced Change

This is where God drew the line in the sand with the Children of Israel. He gave them the 10 plagues to deliver them out of Egypt, He gave them the 10 commandments to get Egypt out of them, and He gave them 10 chances to listen to Him or take action. And, what did they do? They disobeyed Him 10 times, as well as murmured against Him 10 times. God will never violate our will—He wants us to be willing and able to serve Him freely.

As lessons in life avail itself, never force someone or something to change, or it will fight you back, causing war right where the battle started, and that's from WITHIN YOU! If you have not noticed by now, it's human nature to rebel against unwanted change. In spite of your desires to change someone or something, never allow the battle to cause war within your soul. Fighting against yourself about someone or something will cause you to become defeated in many different areas of your life. The **secret** to change is allowing it to be FREE! Allowing someone or something the freedom to change at its own free will is better than forcing an unwanted change to cater to your wants, desires or needs. Change may not occur overnight; however, it will occur when you least expect it. All you need to do is allow it to flow—if it does not flow, there is nothing you can do about it anyway. So, there is no need to stress-out and allow the frustrations of life to destroy your sanity.

The warring power struggles, are no more than your conscience telling you to give up your desire for power, in order to gain strength. You should never engage in a war if you are not strategic about it. Jumping into something without an action plan could be devastating to your well-being. As a matter of fact, a power struggle will only set you up for repetitive mistakes and disappointments. Mistakes and disappointments in life will make you a more meticulous problem solver; however, it means zilch, if you do not take the time to find out the underlying reason for the warring in your spirit. Yes, I agree that some things just happen; however, if you allow your conscience to be your guide—you will always find the lesson behind the happenings as long as you do not whine about it.

Complainer

Complaining is considered to be the junk-food of conversation, it provides little or no added health benefit to those who are partakers of it. Making a statement about something is one thing, but outright complaining is another. Yes, freedom of expression is great; but too much freedom in the way we express ourselves will cause a decline in our health. Most often, our sicknesses are associated with what comes out of our mouth. As a matter of fact, just pay attention, most complainers suffer from high-blood pressure, headaches, backaches, body aches, etc. We are designed to express ourselves; however, in expressing ourselves, we must be able to do just that and move on.

Complainers usually are the ones who often feel as if they

are losing their mind, or feel out of control at times. Not only that, complaining most often is an opinionated, selfish, emotional conversation that is harped about time and time again. Just remember, complaining is a distraction designed to prevent you from putting the past behind you, keep you feeling sorry for yourself, or keep you feeling like a victim. In my opinion, complaining creates the environment or the situation that feed the emotions that drive a person insane. Furthermore, a constant loop of complaining will get an individual tied up with the things that will eventually choke the life out of them. As of today, say what you mean and mean what you say, keeping your conversation positive and to the point where it does not become biased.

CHAPTER 26

The Ancient Secrets Of Life

The issues of life will press us so hard, until we question our relationship with God, just as the Children of Israel did when Moses was unavailable. For this reason, the meeting place is designed for the restoration of your relationship with God and to receive guidance for the rest of the journey. This chapter is very symbolic, and it is going to become the bridge of all the previous chapters creating a dwelling place for the purging of all negativity.

God gave the Children of Israel specific instructions on how to set up the tabernacle, and what to use to build it. He was very strategic and very precise with every aspect of the tabernacle, and its furnishings. Your meeting place is God's way of setting up the reading and the understanding of your life. In chapter 2, I spoke about the importance of prayer; and now, I am sharing with you the **secrets** on how to bring your prayers alive. Actually, this is how you are going to receive daily instructions regarding the way in which you should go—it is your construction site for the building, and the introduction to your Promised Land experience. This is a place (prayer closet) that's just for you—you will meet there for your daily instructions to build the faith that's beyond human understanding, you will also meet there for your daily confession, prayers, and meditation. In this place, you represent the Arc of the Covenant, with the 10 commandments written on the tablet of your heart. Matthew 6:5-6 explains how we should keep our prayers in secret: *And when thou prayest, thou shalt not be as the hypocrites are: for they love to pray standing in the synagogues and in the corners of the streets, that they may be seen of men. Verily I say unto you; They have their reward. But thou, when thou prayest, enter into thy closet, and when thou hast shut thy door, pray to thy Father which is in secret; and thy Father, which seeth in secret, shall reward thee openly.* Now is not the time to get your prayers caught up in the wrong hands, as every moment gives you an opportunity to create your own luck! You are in control of the lessons you learn, and the lessons you don't learn—so if your day is not going the way you anticipate, change your expectations and go to your meeting place. Remember, every day is a blessing in itself, and you create your own miracles by the way in which you think, the way in which you pray, and the PLACE where you pray. Of course, you are able to pray anywhere, as well as on the go, and I do encourage that; however, you must designate a certain place that you call your very own "MEETING PLACE."

In His Presence
What do you do when your life is spinning out of control?

Where do you go when you feel abandoned? Life has a way of asking you questions that need answers—answers that may require you to reevaluate your life. At some point, everyone will have a need for space, some more than others, or just in a different area. Whether you agree with needing your space or not, it is imperative that you take the time out to regroup. The best way to motivate yourself is to take a little time to meditate—taking time out for yourself is one of the greatest hidden **secrets** known to man. As a matter of fact, this is the one thing that we try to avoid. Let's not misunderstand me, keeping busy is good, but keeping too busy will cause a person to ignore some of the answers and divine nudges that come from within. Actually, hearing yourself think is a great way to resolve problems, conflicts, or make decisions. From this day forward, before you talk with anyone else regarding a problem, issue, or decision—talk to yourself first! Just remember, when sorting life out, having your space is a prerequisite for beginning again.

Constant failure in a certain area of our lives should cause us to take a new approach. To keep doing something the same way that ends with the same results of failure will cause even the strongest person to contemplate giving up. Whether you are strong, weak, or anywhere in between— giving up is not an option until you try a new approach. In my opinion, the only person that can destroy you is Y.O.U! God is bigger than any problem you are facing. Don't be afraid to go to Him, for He knows all and He will guide you. If there is a situation with you, in your relationship, with your children or on your job, whatever it may be, place it in His hands and ask Him for a new approach. An effective thought and prayer life will create an environment that allows you to handle the ups and downs without settling for less, or repeating the same failures, over and over again—it's your life, so let's take some time to get it together. God has placed everything we need in our hands; all we need to do is take the time we need to pull the things together and convert them into something positive and productive. The greatest way to do that is in our time of prayer.

Moment of Desperation

In a moment of desperation, prayer in conjunction with faith will carry you through when nothing else will. Praying gives you the ability to confess your thoughts, troubles, weaknesses, sins, strengths, desires, thanksgivings, faithfulness, and dependencies. You do not have to go to college, acquire a special skill or a license to attain dynamic praying abilities—they will come naturally with practice. Praying is very simple; just repent of all sins, ask God for what you need, pray for others and thank Him. If you don't know how to pray, ask God to teach you; if you do not have wisdom, courage or strength, ask for it! You may say at times, "God knows what I need," and you are right—He does know what you need before you ask, but He wants you to know and understand what you need as well.

Open ears and a non-judgmental attitude give us the ability to listen, even when words are not being spoken. Listening to life will provide many invaluable lessons that will enhance the wisdom of all who are willing to avail themselves to partake of it. God will often send us a word of wisdom in the strangest, and the most inconspicuous way possible. All we have to do is, open our ears before we open our mouth, without judging the situation, circumstance, person, place, or thing. Hear me and hear me well, the ability to listen is the most effective way for us to express ourselves and to communicate with others. As a matter of fact, when we stop listening, our relationships with people, places, and things will begin to deteriorate. Yes, there are some things that we may have to turn a deaf ear to; but for the most part, we must allow our conscience to nudge us when the Teacher is trying to speak wisdom into our heart. Trust me; it is hard to hear God when our back is turned away from Him; especially, when listening is the best way to learn from Him. Do me a favor, start listening to the Voice of God, and He will speak to your heart without one word being spoken aloud.

CHAPTER 27

The Real Secret

If you have not gotten the picture by now, I will finally throw you the REAL SECRET. The Children of Israel were not in the desert because they were such bad people, they were not in the desert because they were not prayerful, they were not in the desert because they were murders, they simply lack their biggest downfall, and that was **DISCIPLINE**. When we lack discipline in our lives, we will become a slave to something. As I said earlier, I have zero tolerance for excuses, and I have my reasons. Discipline, happens to be another big one for me as well—I know we all have our own vices; however, we must find a way to bring whatever it is under subjection to bring ourselves out of bondage to safeguard our lineage. If we don't master discipline by this stage in the game, we are doomed to become reckless mentally, emotionally, spiritually, and physically. There some things that money will not be able to buy as far as our mental, emotional, and spiritual well-being. In my opinion, that's the worst type of enslavement that one could ever endure.

The Children of Israel were not the first slaves, nor will they ever be the last. We are a slave to something—although we deny it. We are a slave to Food, Cellphones, Television, Social Media, Sex, Money, Power, Cheating, Friends with Benefits, Smoking, Drinking, Drugs, etc. That is our reality—it is a form of enslavement, and we cannot see it as such; however, the Children of Israel's form of slavery serves as a quick reference guide to ensure that we become released from our temporary enslavement. As we very well know, we all are born into some form of spiritual bondage, and if we can reach beyond our self-imposed limitations to embrace the experience, God will allow us to occupy our own Land of Milk and Honey.

The best way I have found to break free of our bondage is to sit under great leadership and become mentored by them. Environmental conditioning has caused more setbacks than we could care to imagine; therefore, making mantle mentoring extremely important when trying to possess uncharted territory. Remember, each land has their own set of rules; and, if you don't learn them, you will become defeated because your rules will not work on another man's territory—you never enter another man's territory unequipped or uncharted—do your homework. If you don't learn his rules, his game, your rules, your game, God's rules, God's game, and develop a **STRATEGY**—you are going to be defeated every single time! If you are going to run with the **BIG BOYS**, you have to learn how to think like them. It's time out for the cat and mouse, tit for tat games—this is a **GOD RULED NATION**. It tells you that on the Dollar Bill—In God, We Trust; however, that is also why we call the Dollar Bill currency—you have to keep it moving. Spreading, passing it along, sharing, giving, paying it forward, reciprocity, etc., that is the only way you can break a limitation! **Be Warned!** Be careful what you spread—make sure it is goodness, to ensure goodness is coming back to you. Because if you are spreading ill-will, that same Law of Reciprocity is in effect as well. Oh, by the way, make sure you develop a good strategy and not a scheme; schemes have a tendency to backfire on those who are concocting ill-will, especially against God's chosen ones. I am sharing this information for you to do good, and not evil.

Passing the Mantle

As Moses Leadership came to an end, he had to pass it on to Joshua. We can speculate why God chose not to allow Moses into the Promise Land, but there are times when we go through so much drama or turmoil from the past, and it's a possibility God did not want it to carry over into the new territory. However, why Moses did not go to the Promised Land is not the point here! Passing the mantle is the point that I want to drive home. Moses mentored and trained Joshua well enough to take over, lead, and conquer the inhabitants that are in possession of the Promised Land. We as a generation must prepare our youths for a transfer of wisdom, knowledge, and power to carry on our legacy; therefore, producing a continuous cycle of a rotating Promised Land Mantle. We cannot be afraid to transfer the power, vision, and hope into ourselves or successors—we are required to give back! The Law of Reciprocity is a prerequisite for those who desire to reap the harvest and keep the harvest of their Promised Land. Hoarders are not allowed to keep the promises of the seeds of the sower—our blessings are meant to be shared. If they are not, wandering in the wilderness will have all been in vain, and they will begin to curse their seed if they do begin to hoard.

Moses passed the mantle to Joshua showing us that if we do our jobs correctly, when the time is right, our successors will be able to step up to the plate to lead, direct, and conquer without any form of reservation. Along with a disciplined lifestyle, you must become a mentor providing power, vision, or hope back into the legacy of the PROMISE, for it is your reasonable service. You cannot wait until you occupy the land to start sharing information, knowledge, concepts, etc.—you must be doing this on your way in, through the process, occupying, and in your Promise Land.

If it takes you to get you some apprentices, do just that! A little bit goes a long way—you never know the lives that you may inspire by small acts of kindness. It may take years to see the benefits, but trust me it is well worth it. It brings me joy every time I hear a personal testimony of how I inspired someone when they were just a little child; although, I wasn't trying to get any brownie points—I was just being the natural Ruby. However, it brings tears of joy, to see a child go on to become a Doctor, Lawyer, Teacher, Entrepreneur, etc. It will do the same for you as well, when those testimonies start coming back to you—it will make you want to do more, empower more, mentor more, and share more.

If you choose to become a passive mentor, occasional

mentor, or a more involved mentor—do something. If you do not empower another, the knowledge and wisdom that one possess will cause you to implode. That is why the smartest people start breaking down psychologically, and the not so smart people prevail because they are smart enough to share what they have learned from other smart people. That behooves me; but, that is how it works! Therefore, if you learn the laws of how the system works, you too can become SMART! God has created this Universe with Laws, Systems, Strategies, Concepts, and Divine Order; and, if you can wrap your head around that—WISDOM is yours!

When you are a mentor, you must be organized and focused—you cannot be all over the place mentally or emotionally. If you don't know what you are doing—sit yourself down and go back to the drawing board. If you do not have a plan by now, that means that you have skipped the previous chapters, and you need to stop right now, and go back. This is a serious matter—if you are taking your life for granted, that's on you. However, when it comes down to the lives of others, that is not a laughing matter; therefore, I would suggest that you come back to this point when you get a plan together. I take the lives of people seriously; and, in my opinion, leading people in the wrong direction without a plan, a roadmap, or a strategy is considered an atrocity.

When we mentor ourselves and others by, and with the Fruits of the Spirit, it becomes very hard to go wrong in our way and style of mentoring. Although, we all come from a diverse background, and we all are somewhat a byproduct of our environment; however, when we allow the Fruits of the Spirit to govern us—our integrity will stand regardless of where we came from or what we have been through. Do you remember when the 10 spies came back with a bad report, and Joshua and Caleb did not fall into that trap—that's what I am speaking of right now. Regardless, of what anyone says, practice the Good Report of Love, Joy, Peace, Patience, Kindness, Goodness, Faithfulness, Gentleness, and Self-control—trust me; you will touch places in a person's heart that they did not know existed. That is a promise that I will make to you—if you exercise the Fruits of the Spirit when mentoring those in need of what you have to offer. It does not matter if they try to pass judgment, it does not matter if they try to find fault, and it does not matter if they try to set a trap for you—you will still be able to reach them regardless. It will be through your imperfections that they will see the Glory of God work. Trust me on that one! For it is truly through my imperfections that I can pull such powerful information to bring forth to help an imperfect World. Listen to me, it is through the Bread of Life that God feeds me; I turn around with that same piece of bread to feed you; and, I expect you to digest it, and then take it as a Breadcrumb and create a Trail for others to GLEAN from as you occupy the land. You cannot conquer your Promise Land alone; you need a team—I have given you enough information thus far, and you should have enough to get people on your side.

When Passing the Mantle:

- Make sure you are committed to the mentoring process.

- Establish a Vision, Goal, Plan, or Strategy in writing.

- Do not become overbearing; it chases people away.

- Do not become too critical or negative—find a way to create a win-win situation. There is always a positive—find it; I do not care how bad it seems.

- Do not impart fear, teach instincts.

- Teach the consequences and repercussions of making the right or wrong decisions in life.

- Allow flexibility and tolerance for mistakes.

- Exercise patience where experience is needed for the building and molding process.

- Treat this Mentoree relationship as a leadership role.

- Allow the Mentoree to have responsibilities.

- The goal should be to invest, develop, prepare, lead, and mature.

- Find a way to turn a negative into a positive.

- Do not be afraid to bring them in on real negotiations.

- Allow them to become involved in your everyday living and not just business.

- When they have questions, make them provide a road-map of a solution of the What, When, Where, How, and Why's.

- Offer recognition for the growth and maturity process that life requires.

- Offer unconditional love.

- Use your faith to encourage and bring life to all that you come in contact with.

- Exercise kindness in words and deeds.

- Always treat your Mentoree nice exercising integrity in all that you do and say.

- Exercise Godly Principles.

- Offer good advice and encouragement

- Focus on strengths and help the Mentoree to work through their weaknesses.

- Instill confidence in Mentoree.

- Motivate Mentoree to be their best despite the circumstances.

- Evaluate the Mentoree's progress.

- Give feedback to the Mentoree periodically.

- Give the Mentoree a different perspective on life, issues, business, etc.

- Become big on discipline.

- Never make a Mentoree feel neglected, unwanted, or rejected.

Moses had a great impact on the Children of Israel, regardless of whether they found fault in him or not. Most often, we spend many years finding or looking for faults in others, when we should be spending our time enjoying a purposeful life. If the Children of Israel could have just enjoyed life, they would have been so much better off than wandering around in circles for 40 years feeling out of purpose and insecure.

Insecurity causes the best of us to become the worst at being receptive to others with bright, new, and innovative ideas that will benefit us for the better. All too often, people reject the great ideas of others, simply because they do not feel as if they were smart enough, creative enough, or whatever enough to come up with a solution or idea themselves—so they just outright reject what others have to offer. It is best that we do not become a part of the naysayers. If we recognize a great idea, embrace it. If someone is a great inspiration, embrace it. If someone has a great point-of-view, embrace it. If someone does something great or looks great, compliment him or her. Life is too short to reject the greatness of others—it is through their greatness that we are able to shine brightly. Just remember, the greatest inspiration, idea, or concept will come when you least expect it and most often from a person, place, or thing that you would never expect it from.

The Children of Israel allowed the clouds of past defeats to block the true star that God was trying to get them to see. But, no—they allowed anger, fear, rebellion, greed, envy, and bitterness to govern their destiny. Following the star that's in our heart may not always be easy, but it is doable if we believe that it is. As a matter of fact, I have found that if we take a moment to find a star in someone else, it will help illuminate the star that we have from within. If the Children of Israel could have just found a way to appreciate the simple things that God did for them, they would not have suffered the way they did. Though, it may have been harsh; but, if they would have found a way to ask whole-heartedly for mercy and correction—rest assured that it would not have impacted them as bad as it did. Sadly to say, there is no way around the fact that they lacked simple appreciation. In my opinion, the Walls of Jericho in our present day situation represents the Walls that we have placed in our heart, our mind, our soul, and our spirit. We have placed so many walls up in our lives; and we do not allow anyone in, not even God. Although, we put on a big show; however, behind closed doors the truth remains.

When we get to our Promised Land, we must become obedient, marching around that wall in total confidence—trusting and knowing that God will bring that wall down in due time and in due season, whatever that wall is. When He brings that wall down on that issue, situation, circumstance, or event, we must be willing to take possession of our Promise immediately without any form of reservation or doubt. It does not matter what people think, do what has to be done to bring the walls down on that in which is blocking you from your Promise. So what, if people think that you are crazy—they are going to think the same way, if you don't use the tools that are readily available to you to bring down the walls on what rightly belongs to you! When it's time for you to open your mouth, open it and when it's time for you to close your mouth, close it, period. Don't worry about the naysayers, simply respect God, yourself, and then your neighbor.

We will often find people blowing their own trumpets; but we will find that they are blowing their own trumpets for the wrong reasons. If we are blowing our trumpets and not bringing down walls, and possessing the Promises of God, then we must reevaluate what we are doing and the reasons why. What is it all for? Is it about show and tell? I think not—this is about leaving a legacy. If we are not making a difference, if we are not making an impact, if we are not changing lives, then what is this all for? Tell me, Please......I know we cannot save the World; but, I firmly believe that if we can brings some of the walls in our lives down, we can do our share. We can make a difference.

New beginnings start with us making a simple decision to appreciate the people, places, and things in our lives. In order to appreciate the newness of anything, we must become grateful for the things that are present. In so many words, we cannot truly appreciate where we are going until we can appreciate where we are, and where we are not. Yes, we may want this, and we may want that; but, are we really appreciating the "this and that's" of what we have grown accustomed to? For example, we have a person looking for a much newer home—he or she must become a good steward over where they live right now. As they look for a newer home, they must appreciate the difference in each home that they look at. They must also appreciate the potential of the home and what the home is or is not for them. This principle is applicable to every area of our lives, especially in our relationships with people. We must appreciate a person for who they are and respect their differences. Everyone wants something new, but the newness of something is only a thought away. Today, let's start with a new way of thinking. This will definitely bring newness to any situation, circumstance or event that will only enhance our effectiveness to reap more than we have sown or to reap where we haven't sown.

It's a Heart Thing

Knowledge is great, but people do not care about what we know if we are not enthusiastic about it. Of course, some people claim that they don't care about what others think, but when it comes down to paying our bills, keeping a job, keeping our husband/wife/family, etc. All of that is baloney! Our livelihood is important to us, or we would not obtain the knowledge or the know-how to get it in the first place.

Our enthusiasm about what we know comes from the heart. As a matter of fact, it becomes a breadcrumb for our Journey; and, if our heart is not in what we know, then we may have an issue with getting our point across. For example, we have an experience and very knowledgeable professor that teaches straight facts with no enthusiasm, and half of his class always fails, because they fall asleep during his lectures. On the other hand, we have another professor that has been teaching for only a few years, all of his students pass and not only that, they look forward to coming to his class because he has the enthusiasm that's needed to keep his students from falling asleep. So, it is not how much a person knows, it's how enthusiastic they are about what they know, that keeps the attention of others. Not only that, caring about others will put the icing on the cake regarding what you know.

Make no mistake about it; caring is the prerequisite for a truly successful life—it is required for us to love effectively, to give freely, and to create anything of value. As it is often overlooked, caring about others builds Godly character from the inside out. Sadly enough, without our ability to care, we will find that we tend to ignore the fact that we have an inner born desire to care about the wants, needs, and the well-being of others. Today, you can easily start caring for others by asking, "How can I help you?" or "What can I do for you?" This will help eliminate the tendency to become selfish. I have found that this is the quickest way to bring down walls with people who may have built walls around them to protect themselves from those who could care less about them or those who seek to prey on their vulnerability. This is one of **"The Secrets of Life"** that you will never want to forget—helping others with no strings attached is one of the easiest ways to bring down walls with people; and, to keep the wall of SELFISHNESS from forming in your heart. You will thank me later. Trust me on that one!

The Blessing List

When the right opportunity presents itself in our lives, most often we are already prepared for it. If we are not prepared, then God provides help or a mentor to guide us on the journey to prevent us from getting stuck. As a matter of fact, when we maximize our potential to become prepared for what life has to offer—it may consist of us doing the dirty work or doing things that others are not willing to do. The last **secret** in this JOURNEY is, **"LEAVE NO STONE UNTURNED."** This will ensure that the right opportunities do not fall by the wayside, get missed, or overlooked; remember, your blessing will never appear as so—it may be wrapped in a weakness, it may be what others overlook, it may appear as trash, and the list goes on.

Oh, by the way, don't forget to follow up—follow up is key. Hint, hint, it is the follow-up that removes the dust off of hidden opportunities. Let's not become like the Children of Israel, forgetting about what God has done for us in the past—keep track. Developing a motivational or inspirational reference guide of our own, will help us refer back to our reservoir of hope in a time of need. Also, keep a list of your blessings, accomplishments, awards, quotes and not only that, gather some pictures or things that bring you joy—keep all of them in one place. So, when you get fearful or worried take a look at what He has already done for you. Simply keep your reserve system positive, hopeful, full of love and faith. Trust me, when you are in need, having these in your reservoir will create extraordinary strength to overcome or get through anything.

The Ancient Secrets of Life has taken you out of your Egypt, through your desert and into your Promise. You are here—you have made it. Listen closely; it is the Holy Spirit that will guide you the rest of the way. Keep the faith and know that He will never leave you or forsake you. Be Blessed and Be a Blessing to Someone Else.

Ruby Fleurcius